George Wesley Davis

Short-Hand Simplified

A complete text-book on phonography

George Wesley Davis

Short-Hand Simplified
A complete text-book on phonography

ISBN/EAN: 9783337399924

Printed in Europe, USA, Canada, Australia, Japan

Cover: Foto ©Andreas Hilbeck / pixelio.de

More available books at **www.hansebooks.com**

SHORT-HAND ·
· SIMPLIFIED.

A COMPLETE TEXT-BOOK

ON

PHONOGRAPHY,

PRESENTING IN A CLEAR AND CONCISE MANNER
PRINCIPLES BY THE USE OF WHICH PERFECT
LEGIBILITY, AND THE HIGHEST SPEED MAY
BE OBTAINED: ALSO, CONTAINING
A SPECIAL CHAPTER

—: ON :—

CAPITALIZATION AND PUNCTUATION.

BY

GEORGE W. DAVIS.

⸺: ••• :⸺

BUFFALO, N. Y.:
THE BRYANT & STRATTON PUBLISHING CO.,
451 Main Street.
1891.

Preface.

IN PRESENTING this work to the public, the author does so with an earnest conviction that, by its use, a thorough knowledge of short-hand may be obtained with the expenditure of much less time and labor than has heretofore been required.

The logical arrangement of the principles, the simplicity of the rules, and their freedom from exceptions, will insure more correct writing, greater accuracy in reading, and higher speed.

This is not a new system. The material used by the most expert Graham and Pitman phonographers has been carefully arranged and systematized, and presented, free from useless matter, in a clear and concise manner, with illustrations showing the application of each principle.

The "Reporter's Rule of Position" is taught from the very beginning. The Reading and Writing Exercises have been very carefully prepared, and only such words selected as would come under the principles embraced in that lesson, or under those of a preceding one, so that the student learns only those forms for words which he will always use for them. In many text-books one form for a word will be given in one lesson, a second form in another, and perhaps, before the completion of the book, still another form, the pupil becomes confused with the different outlines, does not know which one to use, and is seriously retarded in his progress.

The subject has been very carefully divided into lessons, each one complete in itself, with Reading and Writing Exercises, and questions at the end, by which the student may test his knowledge, and assure himself that he understands the principles therein contained before proceeding to the next lesson.

The engraving has been done by an accomplished artist, and it is hoped that the character of the work will stimulate the student, and result in his acquiring a neat and compact style, which is in every way so desirable.

A special chapter devoted to Capitalization and Punctuation has been added, which will be found a valuable reference by a large majority of those entering upon the duties of a stenographer.

Buffalo, N. Y., May, 1891.

Remarks to the Student.

WHEN YOU ENTER upon the study of Short-hand, do so with a determination to stick to it till you can do good work. If, for any reason, it should take you longer to learn than you expected, remember success will surely follow earnest study and persistent practice. Do not get the erroneous idea that short-hand can be learned only by a talented few. There is nothing of mystery about the art; its principles are simple, and a given degree of proficiency in it can be obtained more quickly than in either grammar or arithmetic.

MASTER EACH LESSON.

If you will accept advice of the utmost importance, you will master each lesson as you proceed, no matter how long it may take you Do this, and you will be surprised at the ease with which short-hand can be learned. Many, in their eagerness to "get through the book," skim over the lessons, and, as a result, get the principles confused; are unable to write correctly; consequently cannot read their notes; soon become discouraged and give it up.

USE GOOD PAPER.

This does not mean expensive paper, but that of a good, firm quality. The slight difference in cost of such paper, and of the soft, flimsy stuff now sold at many of the cheap stationers, will be made up, many times over, in the improved character of the work.

Short-hand note books, opening at the end, can now be secured almost everywhere, and should be used by the student, especially after he has completed the study of the text-book.

Beginners will find the use of double or triple line paper of much assistance in making the consonant strokes of uniform length, and in getting words in their proper positions.

PENCIL, PEN, AND INK.

Many of the best stenographers use a pen altogether; others prefer a pencil. There is little doubt, however, that better and clearer work can be done with a pen than with a pencil. It is well to accustom one's self to the use of both.

When pencils are employed, use a "Stenograph" of medium hardness. It is an excellent plan to have two or three always on hand. Keep them well sharpened, and your outlines will be clear and distinct.

The "Fountain" pen is now largely used, as it can be carried in the pocket as easily as a pencil, and is always ready.

When steel pens are employed, select one suited to your hand. Esterbrook's No. 128, and Gillott's No. 604, F, give excellent results.

Use black ink, and that which flows freely. Poor ink not only gives unsatisfactory results, but seriously retards one's speed.

MANNER OF HOLDING THE PEN.

Hold the pen or pencil between the thumb and first finger, the same as when writing long-hand, except that the face of the pen should be well turned to the left; this will enable one to shade the horizontal characters easily.

SIZE OF CHARACTERS.

Make small outlines; they will insure greater speed and accuracy. About one-eighth of an inch is recommended as the proper length for the consonant strokes. Words should be written about one-fifth of an inch apart.

Contents.

5

ADDITIONAL.

Lesson No. 1.

1. Learn the following phonographic characters.

Phonographic Character.	Consonant it Represents.	Phonographic Character.	Consonant it Represents.
\	p	)	s
\	b	)	z
ǀ	t	⌐	sh
ǀ	d	⌐	zh
∕∕ (called *Chay*)	ch	⌐	l
∕	j	⌐	y
‒	k	) called *Ar*	r
‒ (called *Gay*)	g	∕∕ " *Ray*	
↘	f	⟍	w
↘	v	⌒	m
⟍ as in *thin* (called *Ith*)	th	⌣	n
(as in *then* (called *The*)	th	⌣ (called *Ing*)	ng
		∕∕	h

2.   In phonography the consonants of a word are always written first, the vowels afterwards.

METHOD OF WRITING.

3.   The *l* and *sh* are written both upward and downward. When written upward, *l* is called *Lay;* and *sh*, *Shay*. When written *downward*, *l* is called *El;* and *sh*, *Ish*. Always write *l* upward when standing alone.

4.   Horizontal letters are written from left to right.

5.   The *h* and the straight line for *r* (*Ray*) must always be written *upward*.   All other inclined letters, except *Lay* and *Shay*, are written downward.

6.   *Ray*, being written upward, is more slanting, when standing alone, than *Chay* which is always written *downward*.   They are thus easily distinguishable.

Ray	Chay	Ray-Chay	Chay-Ray	Ray-k	Chay-k

The slant of a stroke may be varied in order to secure a sharper angle, as in *Ray-k*.

—   .

DIRECTIONS.

7.   Repeatedly write the phonographic characters, until they can be formed readily and accurately.   Be careful to make them the same length as here given, about one-eighth of an inch.

8.   Use a fine pen, or a stenographic pencil sharpened to a point.

9. Make the light lines very light, and give just shade enough to the heavy ones to make them distinguishable. Form the letters with one stroke of the pen or pencil; *never go back to touch up a line.*

JOINING CONSONANTS.

10. The pen or pencil should not be lifted in writing any group of consonants; thus,

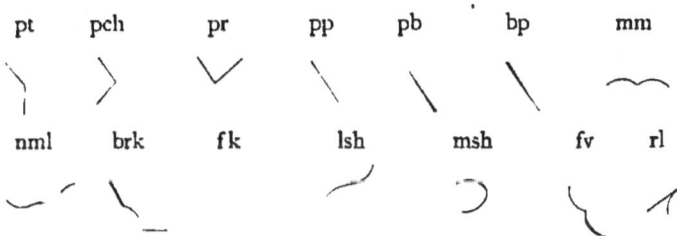

pt	pch	pr	pp	pb	bp	mm

nml	brk	fk	lsh	msh	fv	rl

11. Two or more consonants joined together are called an outline.

READING AND WRITING EXERCISE.

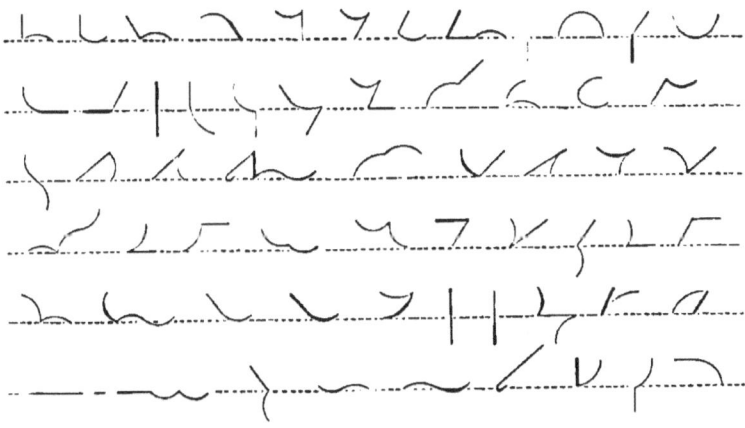

11

12. Read the exercise several times through; then write it over and over, until each outline can be written accurately, and read without hesitation.

QUESTIONS—LESSON No. 1.

1. What letters are written both upward and downward? 2. How may *Ray* and *Chay* be distinguished? 3. In what direction is *h* always written? 4. What is *l* called when written upward? 5. In what direction is *Ray* always written? 6. What is an outline? 7. What length of stroke is recommended for the consonants? 8. In what direction are horizontal letters written?

Lesson No. 2.

WORD SIGNS.

13. On account of the frequent occurrence of certain words, they are provided with brief signs in order that they may be written with the least effort and utmost speed. In the following list, each word is represented by one or more of its leading consonants.

The signs are written in *three* positions; (1) *above the line*, (2) *on the line*, (3) *through or below it*. The hyphen indicates that the sign stands for two words; thus, *thank-ed* represents both thank and thanked.

. . . .	hope		. . . . . .	them or they
. . . .	be		. . . . .	though or thou
. . . .	to be		. . . .	use or us
. . . .	it		. . . .	was
. . . .	do		. . use, (pronounced *uze*)
. . . .	had		. . . .	wish or she
. . . .	which		. . . . . .	shall or shalt
. . . .	much		. . . .	usual-ly
. . . . . .	advantage		. . . . . .	will or wilt

13

-- /	. . . . large	--⌒	. . . . whole
—	. . . common, kingdom	⋯⋯	. . . . . . her or hear
⋯7.	. . . . commonly	⋯)	. . . . are
⋯⋯	. . . . come	⋯⌒⋯	. . . . am or him
—	. . . . . . give or given	⋯⋯	. . . . home
⋯—	. . . . together	⌣	. . . . any or in
↘.	. . . . for	⌣	. . . . own
↘	. . . . ever	⌣	. . . . thing
↘	. . . . have	⌣.	. . . . language
↘.	. . . . however	⌐	. . . . why
(_	. . . . think	⋯)⋯	. . . . away
⋯(⋯	. . . . . . thank-ed	⌐_	. . . . your

14. The above list should be written until every word can be expressed by its proper sign, and in its proper position, at the rate of at least *fifty a minute*. The ability to read the signs with equal rapidity after they have been written, is also very important.

VOWELS.

15. Vowels are represented by light and heavy dots, and by light and heavy dashes. These are written in three positions *beside* the consonant strokes, viz.: in the *first* place, or opposite the *beginning;* in the *second* place, or opposite the *middle;* and in the *third* place, or opposite the *end.*

LONG VOWELS—HEAVY DOTS AND DASHES.

Sound	Sign		Sound	Sign	
ē	•	. . . . as in *eat*	aw	⁻,	. as in *all* or *law*
ā	•	. . . . as in *ale*	ō	⁻,	. . as in *oat, old*
ah.	. . ,	. . . . as in *Ma*	ōō	_	. . . as in *mood*

16. The *T* stroke in the above, merely serves to indicate the position of the vowel but is no part of it.

17. The dots and dashes do not represent *letters*, but *sounds*. For instance, the heavy dot opposite the beginning represents only the long sound of *e*, as in *eat, eel*, etc. When *e* has the short sound (*eh*), as in *ell, fed, her*, etc., it is represented by a different sign as noted hereafter.

18. In learning the vowels, remember the words given as examples ; they will serve as " keys " in case of doubtful sounds.

19. Since *Lay, Ray*, and *h* (and sometimes *sh*) are written upwards, the first place vowels will be at the *bottom* of these strokes; thus, ·

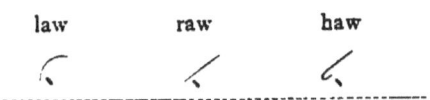

law   raw   haw

20. All words are spelled by *sound*, and all silent letters are omitted.

METHOD OF PLACING THE VOWELS.

21. A vowel, to be read before a consonant, must be placed *above* a horizontal stroke, or at the *left* of any other.

A vowel, to be read after a consonant, must be placed *below* a horizontal stroke, or at the right of any other.

POSITION OF WORDS.

22.   The consonant outlines of words are written in three positions, according as the vowel—or, if more than one, the accented vowel—is first, second, or third place.   *The first position is above the line ; the second position is on the line ; the third position, for perpendicular and inclined strokes, through the line ; and for horizontals below it ;* thus,

peak   became   boom   coo

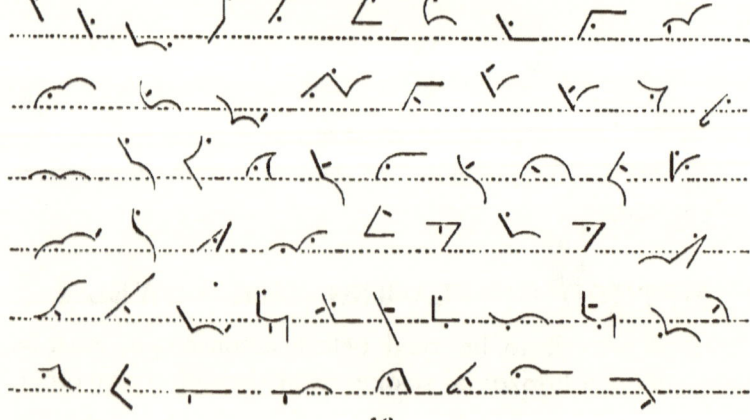

23.   When a word is composed of both horizontal, and perpendicular or inclined strokes, the *first perpendicular* or *inclined* stroke should be written in the place denoted by the accented vowel ; thus,

keep   Dakota   move   veto   Bailey

· READING EXERCISE.

16

24. The foregoing, and all subsequent exercises, should be gone over until they can be read quickly and accurately. The most rapid progress will be made by him who *masters* every principle and exercise as he goes along, and *reviews frequently* all that he has been over.

WRITING EXERCISE.

Write the following words in their proper positions, taking care to make the consonants the same size as those in the Reading Exercise. Make the heavy dots and dashes with one stroke of the pen or pencil. *Never go over a line.* This, and each subsequent exercise, should be written from forty to fifty times.

Page, mole, pool, meal, ale, peach, reach, rope, aim, may, each, palm, came, woo, shaw, shoo, key, league, shame, leeway, fear, oath, Esau, thaw, obey, joke, peep, beam, dome, doom, meek, teem, cape, leave, below, Zeno, gnaw, dough, awed, knave.

QUESTIONS—LESSON No. 2.

1. How are the vowels represented? 2. What represents the sound of a? 3. Of *ah*? 4. Of *aw*? 5. In how many positions are the vowels written? 6. Where is the first position? 7. Where must a vowel be placed to be read before a consonant stroke? 8. What is the third position for perpendicular or inclined strokes? 9. For horizontals? 10. In case a word is composed of both horizontal, and perpendicular or inclined strokes, which would be written in the position denoted by the accented vowel? 11. Do the dots and dashes represent letters or sounds?

Lesson No. 3.

LIGHT VOWELS.

Sound.	Sign.		Sound	Sign.	
I .	｜ . .	as in *it*	ŏ ,	. ‾	as in *on* and *odd*
ė (*eh*) . .	⌐｜ .	as in *Ed* and *her*	ŭ ,	‾｜	as in *up*
å	｜	as in *at*	ŏŏ . . .	‾｜ . . .	as in *foot*

25. The same rules apply to both long and short vowels. Repeat the sounds both forward and backward, until they can be given quite rapidly.

VOWELS BETWEEN STROKES.

26. When a vowel occurs between two consonant *strokes* it should be written: (1) After the first stroke, if it is a *first place*, or *long second place* vowel; thus,

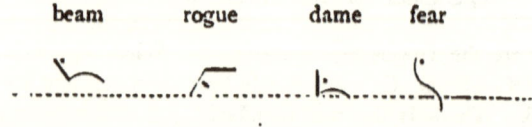

| beam | rogue | dame | fear |

18

(2.) Before the second stroke, if it is *third place*, or a *short second place* vowel ; thus,

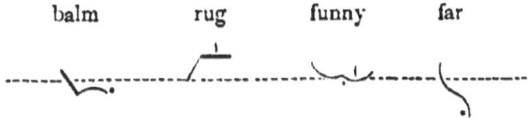

balm   rug   funny   far

27. The above rule should not be used when its observance would bring a vowel into an angle, as in *camera ;* the main object of the rule being to keep the vowels out of the angles.

DIPHTHONGS.

Sound.	Sign.		Sound.	Sign.	
i	˅|	. as in *ice* and *by*	*ou* . . .	˄|	. as in *out* and *owl*
oy	˄|	. as in *oil* and *boy*	*ew* . . .	⊲|	. as in *due* and *hue*

28. The diphthongs are written in the first and third positions only. They are governed by the same rules as the vowels.

29. When two vowels, or a vowel and a diphthong, occur between two consonant strokes, it is advisable, whenever possible, to place one to each stroke ; thus,

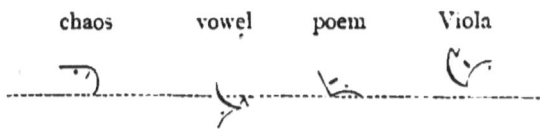

chaos   vowel   poem   Viola

30. The direction and position of the diphthongs are never changed.

31.   When convenient, *i* and *oy* may be joined at the beginning, and *ou* and *ew* at the end of consonant strokes.

32.   When two vowels, or a vowel and a diphthong, have to be written to one consonant stroke, the one which comes next to the consonant should be written nearest to it ; thus,

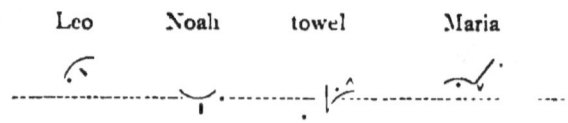

Leo   Noah   towel   Maria

THE PRONOUN I.

33.   *I,* when standing alone, may be represented by the diphthong *i,* or, better, by a light, perpendicular tick *above* the line.

1.   When joined to a *following* word, the tick takes the direction of *p* or *Chay*.

2.   When joined to a *preceding* word, the tick takes the direction of *t* or *k.*

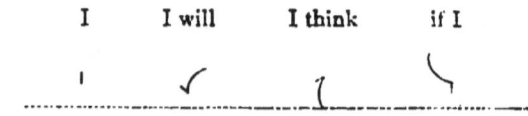

I   I will   I think   if I

3.   Remember that *I,* when standing alone, or when joined to a following word, must be *above* the line.

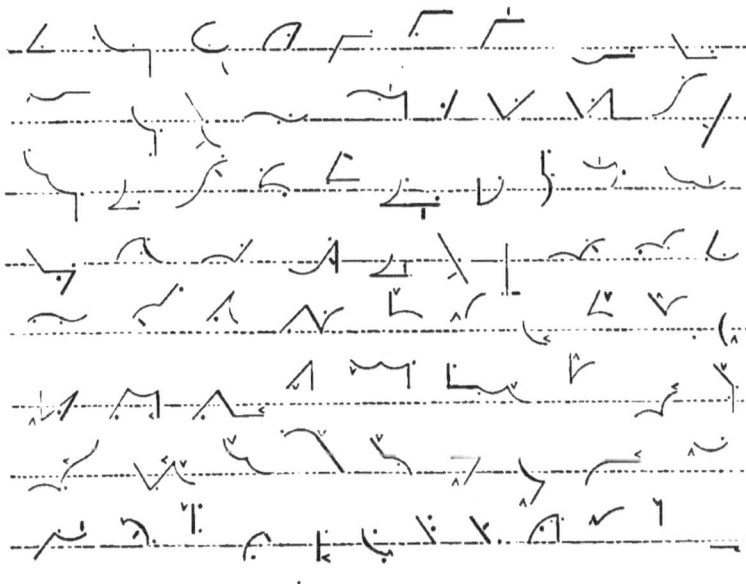

WRITING EXERCISE.

Fussy, shuck, gash, cash, shaky, gummy, bevy, putty, vivify, veto, bank, gang, cook, gag, gage, catch, bath, Fanny, boom, fang, abed, bung, tongue, many, aback, budge, coke, life, tiny, beauty, cue, bellow, Philo, Mary, muddy, puny, item, fume, adieu, Sue, annoyed, denude, Zion, cubic, Noah, Ohio, Genoa, assume, knife, voyage, dial, oceanic, bayonet.

VOWEL WORD SIGNS.

all	already awe	ought	of	or	on
\	ı	/	\	ı	ʹ /

too	oh	who			
two	owe	whom	to	but	should

34. The dashes should be made only one-fourth the length of a consonant stroke.

QUESTIONS—LESSON No. 3.

1. Where should third place vowels be written when occurring between two consonant strokes? 2. Heavy second place? 3. First place? 4. How long should the dash Vowel word-signs be made? 5. What is the difference between the diphthong signs for *i* and *oy*? 6. In what direction does the sign for *ew* point? 7. When two vowels occur between consonant strokes, how is it customary to write them? 8. When two vowels have to be written beside one consonant stroke, how do you denote which is read first?

Lesson No. 4.

—

35. On account of the frequent occurrence of *s* and *z*, a brief sign is provided in the small circle, which is used for either *s* or *z*.

36. No confusion will result from employing the small circle for both *s* and *z*, as the context will readily show which one was intended.

37. The small circle is called *Iss*, to distinguish it from the stroke, which is called *Es*.

38. When joined at the beginning or end of a straight line, the circle should be made with a *left* motion—contrary to that of the hands of a watch ; thus,

Iss-T   T-Iss   Iss-K   Iss-Ray   Iss-H   Iss-H-Iss

39. When joined at the beginning of *h*, the hook is made into a circle, thus forming an exception to the foregoing rule. See preceding illustration.

Iss-h is never used for *sh* unless a vowel occurs between the *s* and *h*.

23

40. When joined at the beginning or end of a curve, the circle is written on the *concave* (inner) side ; thus,

Iss-f   The-Iss   M-Iss   Ar-Iss   Lay-Iss

41. When the circle occurs between strokes, it should be written in the most convenient manner ; thus,

Ray-Iss-K   M-Iss-N   N-Iss-M   F-Iss-Lay-T   F-Iss-El

Between two *straight* lines, the circle will come *outside* the angle.

ST, STR, SEZ.

42. *St* may be represented by a small loop, *called Steh*, joined at the beginning or end of any consonant stroke: thus,

Steb-T   F-Steb   state   boast   fast   rest

43. A circle or loop at the beginning of an outline is read *first*, at the end of an outline, *last*.

44. *Str* may be represented by a large loop, called *Ster;* thus,

faster   rooster   Hester   pastor   master   duster

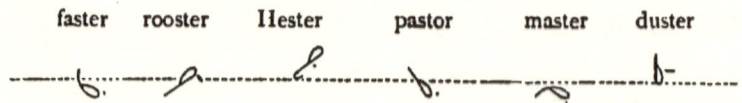

1. The large loop is never joined at the *beginning* of a word.

45. *The large circle*, called *Sez*, is used to represent two *s* or *z* sounds, with a vowel between them, usually forming a syllable; as *sys*, *sus*, *sis*, etc.; thus,

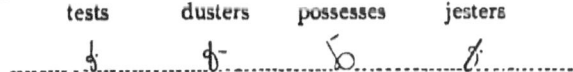

| system | Susan | desist | races |

1. The vowel is written inside the circle without regard to position

2. It is unnecessary to insert the vowel when the circle comes at the end of a word. A little practice will enable the student to omit it altogether.

46. The small circle may be added to the loops, and to the large circle; thus,

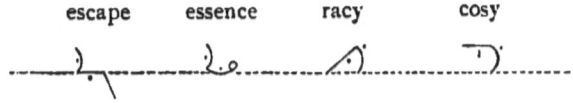

| tests | dusters | possesses | jesters |

47. The small loop is also used to represent the *sound* of final *st*, and *zt*, as heard in *passed*, *raced*, *amazed*, *dazed*, etc.

1. It should be noticed that many words ending with *d* take the sound of *t*, as *passed*, *raced*, etc.

USES OF S AND Z.

48. Use the strokes in the following cases :

1. When *s* or *z* *follows* an *initial* or *precedes* a *final* vowel, as in

| escape | essence | racy | cosy |

2.   At the beginning of a word, when two sounded vowels follow, or when *s* or *z* would be the only stroke consonant in the word.

science   seance   sayings   sciatica   cease   seize

Also in compound words formed from *sea*, as *sea-sick*,
sea-service, etc.

3.   At the end of a word, when two sounded vowels
precede, as in *bias*, *chaos*, etc.

4.   When the sound of *z* begins a word it must be represented by a *z* stroke; thus,

zest   zeal   zenith   Zona

(*a.*)   Use the circle in all other cases.

READING EXERCISE.

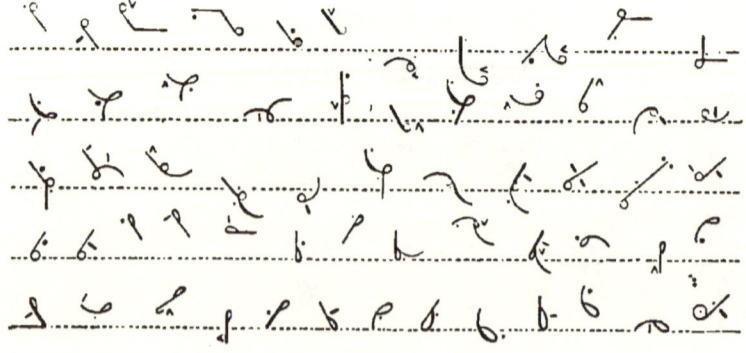

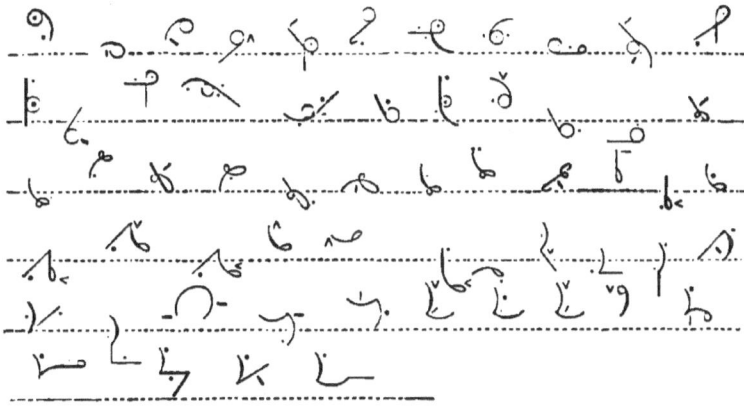

WRITING EXERCISE.

Soup, spoke, abuse, revise, device, obtuse, shows, mason dusk, suppose, palms, seal, loosely, dispose, sketches, schemes, cousin, pathos, chosen, missile, yes, husky, shies, oils, Silas, spies, mouse, step, just, nest, stake, stoop, steal, stools, stoops, yeast, stout.

Pastor, pester, taster, roaster, castor, coaster, Lester, Baxter, Rochester, Custer, lustre, vases, adduces, loses, houses, voices, saucer, sausage, doses, season, exercise. disease, necessaries, insist, successive, devices.

Chests, rests, costs, roasts, exercises, abscesses, diseases, tasters, excesses, bossed, paused, effaced, encased, voiced, housed, kissed, missed, appeased, noosed, asp, assist, asks, Asa, easy, oozy, easily, mazy, gauzy, lazy, mossy, lessee, lasso, Jesse, seaside, Zeno.

QUESTIONS—LESSON No 4.

1. What is used as a brief sign for *s* and *z*? 2. A circle or loop at the beginning of an outline is read when? 3. At the end of an outline? 4. How should a circle be written when joined at beginning or end of a straight line? 5. When it occurs between two strokes? 6. Where will the circle come when it occurs between two straight lines? 7. What does the large circle represent? 8. The large loop represents what? 9. Is the large loop ever joined at the beginning of a stroke? 10. Give the rules for the use of the *s* and *z* stroke.

Lesson No. 5.

USES OF AR AND RAY AT THE BEGINNING OF A WORD.

49.   1.   After an *initial* vowel use the *curve* sign for *r* when it is the only stroke consonant, also after an initial vowel when followed by *p, b, k, g, r, s, m, n, l*, or *sh;* thus,

array	orb	arm	error	arise

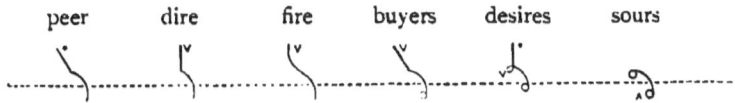

2.   Also for *r* preceding *m* in such words as,

Rome	farm	disarm	remiss	resume

3.   *Ray* should be used in nearly every other case.

————

AT THE END OF A WORD.

50.   1.   Use the curve sign for *final r*, unless the preceding *stroke* is *th, m*, or *Ray*.

2.   Also for final *rs*, when no vowel occurs between the *r* and *s;* thus,

peer	dire	fire	buyers	desires	sours

3.   Use *Ray* in other cases.

29

R BETWEEN STROKES.

51. The general rule is to use *Ray* if a vowel follows, and *Ar* if one does not. When difficult junctions, or loss of speed would result, use whichever may be most convenient. *Ray* should follow *m*, *th*, and *Ray* in all cases.

52. The foregoing rules are very important, and should be so thoroughly memorized that they can be applied *without hesitation*. A careful observance of them will insure uniformity of writing, ease of reading, and greater speed.

READING EXERCISE.

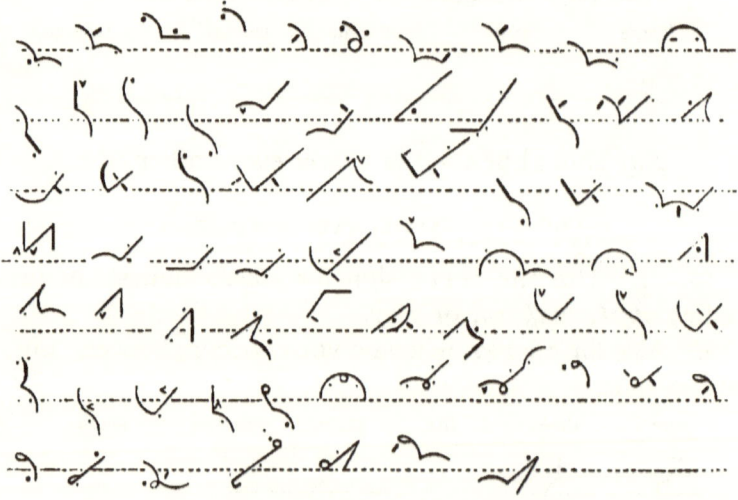

WRITING EXERCISE.

Mirror, ark, arch, Aurora, curry, berry, bar, rack, rarer, arrow, furry, four, jury, rum, urge, rich, rake, wretch, rash, shower, sower, arena, renew, irate, arnica, aright, Arabic,

oriole, irony, relay, rag, rainy, ramify, rapier, sherry,
ream, bureau, nigher, marrow, bar, roar, wrong, rebuke,
Peru, Darrow, Verona, remedy, steamer, source, barrier,
furrier, soar, erased, store, story, lures.

QUESTIONS—LESSON No. 5.

1. What name is given to the straight line for *r*? 2. What name is
given to the curved sign? 3. Is the straight line written upward or downward? 4. Which sign is used when *m* follows? 5. What is said about
the use of *r* between strokes? 6 Give rule for the use of *r* at the beginning of a word? 7. The curved stroke is generally used for final *r*, except
when preceded by what three consonant strokes?

Lesson No. 6.

—

USES OF EL AND LAY AT THE BEGINNING OF A WORD.

53. 1. The *downward* stroke should generally be used when *l* is preceded by an *initial* vowel, and followed by any consonant that can be conveniently joined, usually *k*, *g*, *m*, *n*, *Iss-n*, *Ing*, or *j* ; thus,

alike   Elma   allege   alum

2. The downward *l* may also be used to advantage for *initial l*, when followed by *n*, *Iss-n*, or *Ing* ; thus,

Leon   lessen   lung   lank

3. Use *Lay* in all other cases.

——

L AT THE END OF A WORD.

54. 1. The downward stroke should generally be used for *final l*, when preceded by any consonant that can be conveniently joined, usually *f*, *v*, *n*, *Ing*, *k*, *g*, or *Ray* ; thus,

file   vale   Nile   snail   scowl

2. After *n* and *Ing* use the down stroke, whether a vowel follows or not.

3. Use *Lay* in all other cases.

L BETWEEN STROKES.

55. Use whichever one will give the better junction.

USES OF ISH AND SHAY.

56. *Ish* is written downward, and *Shay*, upward.

57. 1. *Shay* is generally used when preceded or followed by *l*, as in *lash* or *shell*.

2. *Shay* is generally used when preceded by *t*, *d*, or *f*.

3. *Ish* is used in nearly every other case.

READING EXERCISE.

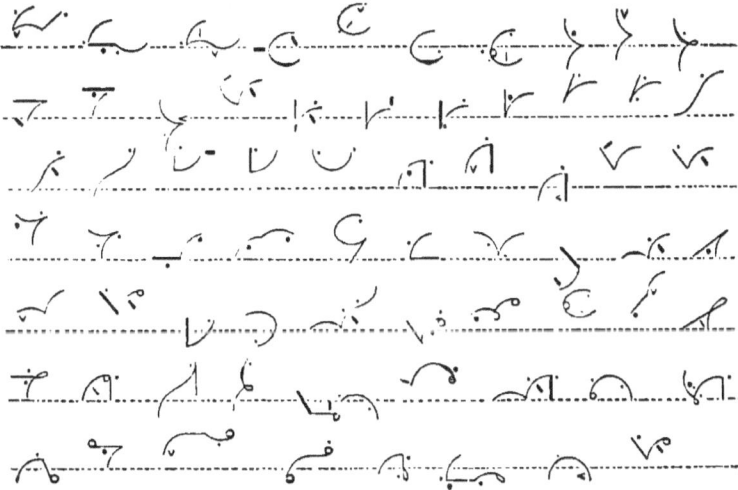

WRITING EXERCISES.

Malay, alchemy, relay, lace, bell, feel, slack, lame, knoll, poll, pale, gull, mealy, kneel, slash, fowl, ideal, elbow, allayed, loath, thill, ledge, allure, scale, abolish, foil, excels, laces, looser, alimony, fizzle, muzzle, lustre, slashed, assail, counsel, Basil, elm, alarm, solicit, solve, solitary, reveal, comely, tile, weasel, wisely. police, alack, billow, illness, null, polish, elope, alibi, Elias, cowl, viol.

- ——

QUESTIONS—LESSON No. 6.

1. What is the name of the downward stroke for *l*? 2. What is the name of the upward stroke? 3. *El* should be used at the beginning of an outline when? 4. What is the rule for the use of *El*, final? 5. What is said of *l* between strokes? 6. What is *sh* called when written downward? 7. When written upward? 8. When *sh* is followed by *l*, should *Ish* or *Shay* be used? 9. Which should be used when *l* precedes *sh*? 10. Which should be used when *sh* follows *t* or *d*?

Lesson No. 7.

H REPRESENTED BY A DOT.

58.   A convenient method of representing *h* before a vowel, is by a light dot written beside the vowel; thus,

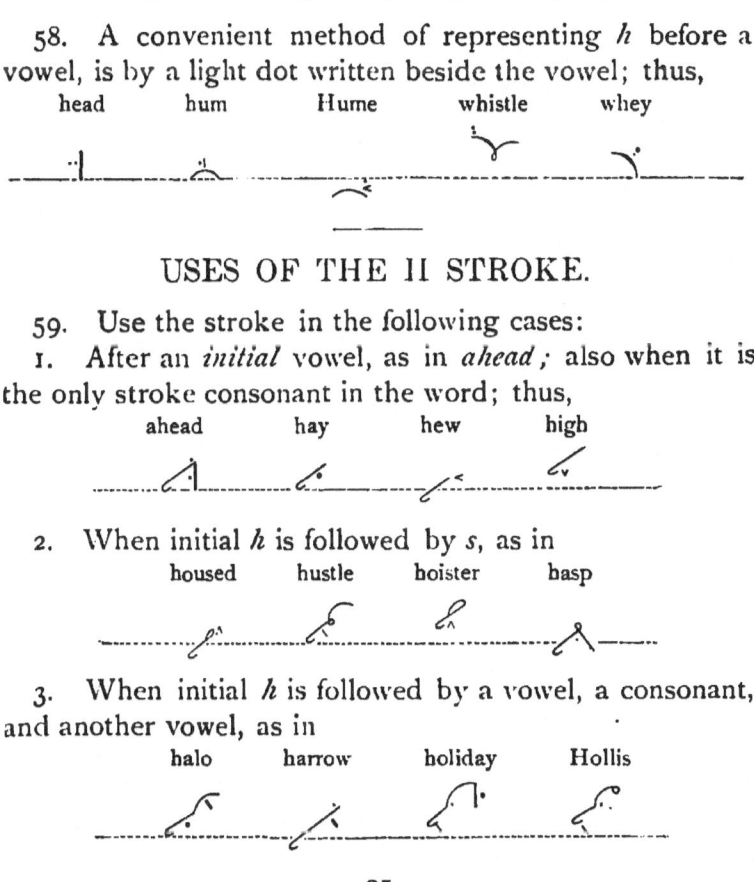

USES OF THE H STROKE.

59.   Use the stroke in the following cases:

1.   After an *initial* vowel, as in *ahead;* also when it is the only stroke consonant in the word; thus,

2.   When initial *h* is followed by *s*, as in

3.   When initial *h* is followed by a vowel, a consonant, and another vowel, as in

Also when followed by two vowels, as in *Howell, haying,* etc.

4.   For initial *h* in the past tense of verbs of one syllable (unless *m* follows *h*); as in *hugged, hacked, heaped, heated,* etc.

60.   Experienced writers almost invariably omit the *h-dot.* When deemed necessary, the vowel following the dot is inserted.   This, together with the context, is sufficient to indicate the word.

The student, from the beginning of his writing, should omit the dot, at least from all familiar words, and he will soon be able to read without it.

61.   Occasional cases may arise where a departure from the rules for the use of *l, r, h,* etc., will give some special advantage in joining, in speed, or in the forming of derivatives; but the rules here given will be found to cover, in the best manner, nearly every case.

THE, A, AN, & AND.

62.   *The,* when standing alone, should always be represented by a light *dot* in the first position.   *The* may be joined to a *preceding word* by a light *tick,* written in the direction of *p* or *Chay;* thus,

for the   bakes the   knows the   which the   show the

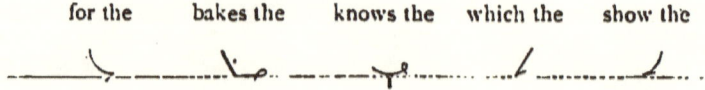

63. *A*, when standing alone, is represented by a heavy dot on the line. *A* may be joined at the beginning or end of any word, by a light *perpendicular* or *horizontal* tick, thus,

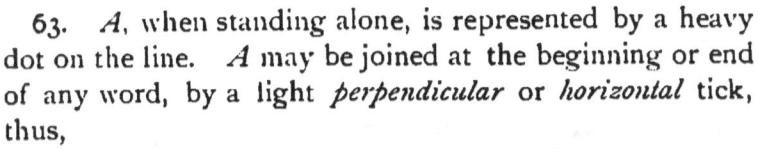

for a   in a   a face   a newsboy   ate a

64. *An* or *and*, when standing alone, is represented by a light dot on the line. Either may be joined at the beginning or end of words, by a *perpendicular* or *horizontal* tick, the same as *a*.

TICK FOR HE.

65. The pronoun *he* is represented by a light tick *on the line*, written in the direction of *p* or *ch*. It may be joined to a preceding or following word; thus,

he will   he may   for he   he should   should he

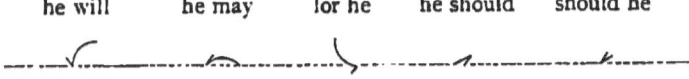

READING EXERCISE.

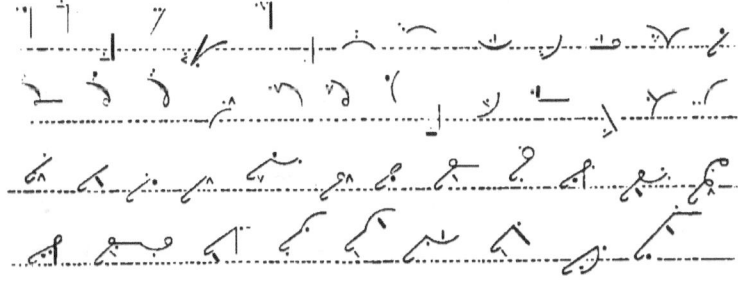

448402

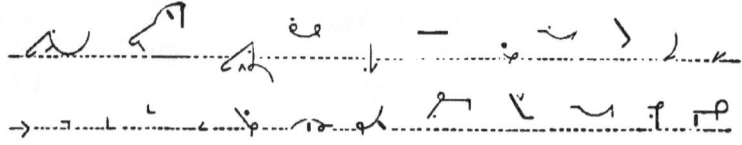

WRITING EXERCISE.

Hops, hooks, hacks, hawks, hoed, ham, hate, heel, whew, wheezes, hedge, Hicks, hums, hunks, hank, halves, hubs, hoops, hides, hang, huckster, horseshoe, Ohio, hoes, Hyson, hussar, Harris, hazy, hyacinth, hurried, housetop, hostile, horrify, horrid, harassed, highway, hissing, hobby-horse, honey-box, pass the, wish the, leave the, fix the, but the, and should, should an, owe a.

WORD SIGNS—CONTRACTIONS.

. . . . several	. . refers or reference
. . . . . . because	. . . . highly
. . . . . . subject-ed	. . . . notwithstanding
. . . . this	. . . nevertheless
. . . . those or thus	. . . . . object-ed
. . . . . . is or his	. . . . . objector
. . . . . . as or has	. . . . . peculiar-ity
. . . . first	. . . . . irregular-ity
. . . . . . .influence	. . . . . regular-ity
. . . . . . influences	. . . . . . something

38

⌣ . . . . influenced	◁ . . . . represent-ed
⟋ . . . . . . acknowledge	⌐ . . . . nothing
⌣ . . . . anything	⊃ . . . . . . is as, or is his
⌐ . . . . knowledge	○ . . . . . his is, or his has
⟍ . . . . become	⌐ . . . . . as his, or as is
♭ . . . . . . disadvantage	⌐ . . . . has his, or has as
⌐ . . . . never	⌐ . . . . now
⟍ . . . . familiar-ity	⌣ . . . . new
⟋ . . . . refer-red	⌐ . . . . forever

QUESTIONS—LESSON No. 7.

1. How many ways are there of representing *h*? 2. Give the rules for the use of the *h* stroke. 3. When is *Iss-h* used? 4. Is it usually necessary to write the dot for *h*? 5. How is the word *the* represented when written alone? 6. May the tick for *the* be joined to following words? 7. *A*, when standing alone, is represented how? 8. ' May *a* be joined to both preceding and following words? 9. What distinction is there between the tick for *the* and the tick for *a, an* or *and*?

Lesson No. 8.

BRIEF SIGNS FOR W.

66. For convenience and speed, *w* is represented by three brief signs, the hook, and two semi-circles, called

Weh   Wuh

c   ɔ

THE W HOOK.

67. *W* may be joined as a hook to five strokes : *Lay*, *El*, *Ray*, *m*, and *n ;* thus,

wail	welcome	queer	we may	twain

WEH AND WUH.

68. These signs may be joined to any consonant (except *h*) not taking the *W* hook.

(*a*) Use whichever will give the better junction, usually *Weh*. The sign should form an *angle* with the consonant to which it is joined ; thus,

wash	weak	Waith	wade	wing

40

ISS JOINED TO BRIEF W.

69. The small circle may be joined to *Weh* and *Wuh*,
and to the *W hook* on *Ray ;* thus,

switch unswayed   swirl

(*a*) A slight flattening of the circle when so added will
produce easier joinings and better results.

GUIDE TO THE USE OF THE W-HOOK.

70. Use the Hook in the following cases .
1. For *initial w* when followed by *l*, *r*, *m*, or *n*.
2. For *initial sw* preceding *r*.
3. For *w* between two consonants, the second of which
is *Lay*, *Ray*, *m*, or *n*, providing the hook can be easily
joined.

GUIDE TO USE OF WEH AND WUH JOINED.

71. Use *Weh* and *Wuh* joined :
1. For *initial w*, unless followed by the consonants, *l*,
r , *m*, *n*, *s*, or *z*, or the combinations, *fl*, *tl*, *pr*, *chr*, etc.
2. When initial *sw* is followed by *t*, *d*, *Chay*, *j*, *f*, *v*, or
Ish.
3. Sometimes in the middle of a word, as in *inweave*.

BRIEF SIGNS FOR Y.

72. *Y* has two brief signs :
 Yeh, opening upward, and *yuh*, opening downward.

◡   ◠

73. Use *Yeh* or *Yuh* as is most convenient, but join so as to form an angle with the consonant to which it is attached ; thus,

yon	yell	unyoke	youngster	Yates

74. *Yeh* and *Yuh* are usually joined for initial *y*, unless followed by *s*, but rarely for *y* between strokes.

75. The foregoing rules for the use of Brief *W* and *Y*, refer to these signs when *joined to* the consonant strokes. In a following chapter they will be given disjoined. Care must be taken not to get them confused. Let these be thoroughly mastered before proceeding further.

READING EXERCISE.

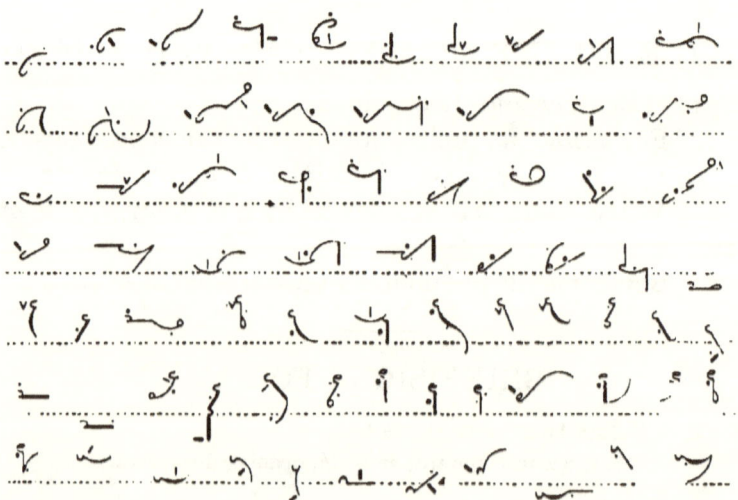

42

WRITING EXERCISE.

Well, wall, wheel, whale, war, wiry, warlike, windy, twin, wealthy, worse, Welsh, whine, whence, wines, wiles, unworthy, unwearied, quarry, wearily, weaver, warp, warmth, warwhoop, warty, welfare, wheat, wad, white, weaknesses, whitewood, waxes, waggish, waive, wallower, walk, whack, wingless, whip, white-cap, whitewash, white-wine, whiteness, wood-house, swarthy, sweat, sweetness, swearer, sweet-wood, sweetish, yellow, yacht, yam, Eunice, yawns.

QUESTIONS—LESSON No. 8.

1. *W* has how many brief signs? 2. What is the one called opening to the right? 3. To what strokes may the hook be joined? 4. To the *W hook* on what letter may the small circle be joined? 5. Give the rules for the use of the hook? 6. How must *Weh* and *Wuh* be joined to the consonant strokes? 7. How many brief signs has *y?* 8. How must they be joined to the strokes?

Lesson No. 9.

USES OF THE W STROKE.

76. Use the stroke for *w:*

1. When it is the only consonant in the word.

2. After an initial vowel :—

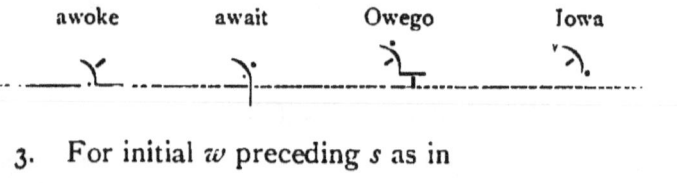

| awoke | await | Owego | Iowa |

3. For initial *w* preceding *s* as in

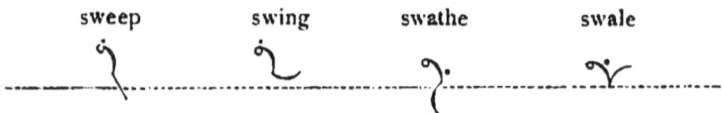

| waste | wiser | wisely | whiskey |

4. For *w* following initial *s*, they being the only consonants, or being followed by any stroke (*r* excepted) that can be easily joined, usually, *p, b, k, g, th, l, m, n, ng ;* thus,

| sweep | swing | swathe | swale |

77. The use of the stroke will also be found convenient when *w* is followed by *fl, vl, dl, pr,* etc., as in *waffle, weevil, sweeper,* etc., explained in a following chapter.

44

USES OF THE Y STROKE.

78. Use the *Y* stroke in the following cases:

1. When it is the only stroke-consonant in the word, or when it is followed by *s*, as in *yes, yeast*, etc.

2. When it follows an initial vowel, as in *oyer*.

BRIEF W AND Y IN THE VOWEL PLACES.

79. *W* or *Y*, and a following vowel, may often be advantageously represented by writing brief *W* or *Y* in the place of the vowel; thus,

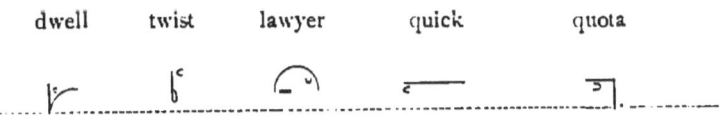

dwell   twist   lawyer   quick   quota

80. *W* and *Y*, and a following diphthong, may be treated the same as *W* and *Y* and a following vowel.

81. Brief *W* or *Y*, may be joined to the diphthong, signs.

82. If the vowel following the *w* or *y* is a dot vowel, use *Weh* or *Yeh* as the case may be; if it is a dash vowel, use *Wuh* or *Yuh;* thus,

we or wĭ	ᶜ	waw or wŏ	ɔ	yĕ or yĭ	ᵙ	yaw or yŏ	ʌ
way or wĕh	ᶜ	wŏ or wûh	ɔ	yă or yĕh	ᵛ	yŏ or yûh	ʌ
wah or wă	ᶜ	wŏŏ or wŏŏ	ɔ	yah or yă	ᵙ	yŏŏ or yŏŏ	ʌ

83. The semi-circles may be shaded for the long vowels if great accuracy is required. This distinction, however, is regarded as wholly unnecessary.

84. **The Brief W Disjoined,** is used principally for *w* between consonants, where the hook, or semi-circle, could not be joined to advantage; as in *twist, dwell, quick,* etc.

85. **Brief Y Disjoined,** is used comparatively little, it generally being considered preferable to join (§ 86 excepted) where the junction will permit.

86. Brief *y* may also be advantageously employed to represent two vowel sounds, the first of which is *i* or *e;* thus,

yä for *ia,* as in *opiate* . . . .

yäh " *iu,* " *various* . . . .

yō " *io,* " *inferior* . . . .

ya " *ia,* " *Arabia* . . . .

87. While the employment of brief *Y,* as above illustrated, does not exactly represent the vowel sounds, it so nearly does so, as to fulfill all requirements, and result in the saving of one vowel, and sometimes one stroke consonant, as in the word *various.*

PUNCTUATION, PROPER NAMES, ACCENT, ETC.

88. **Punctuation.** The following are all the punctuation marks commonly used in shorthand notes:

Period . . . .　 / or x

Interrogation . . . .　 / or ?

Parenthesis . . . .　 ( )

Dash . . . .　 ~~~

89. If other punctuation is desired, the ordinary characters may be used

90. **Proper Names or Capital Letters,** may be indicated by placing two lines beneath the name or character ; thus,

Jennie   James H. Cope   Illinois

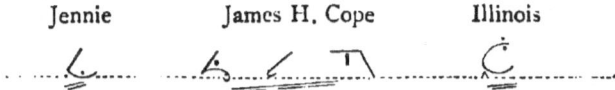

91. **Emphasis** may be indicated, as in longhand, by drawing one or more lines under the emphasized word.

92. **Accent** may be indicated by placing a small cross near the accented vowel ; thus,

August   august

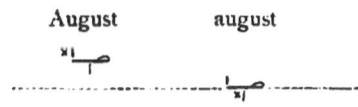

WORD-SIGNS—CONTRACTIONS.

. . . . we or with	. . . we will, or while
. . . . were	. . . . we are
. . . . what	. . . . where
. . . . would	. . . . aware
. . . . ye	we may, or with me
. . . . yet	. . . when, or we know
. . . . beyond	. . . . whenever
. . . . you	. . . . wherever

47

NOTE:—*We*, beginning a phrase, always takes the first position.

READING EXERCISE.

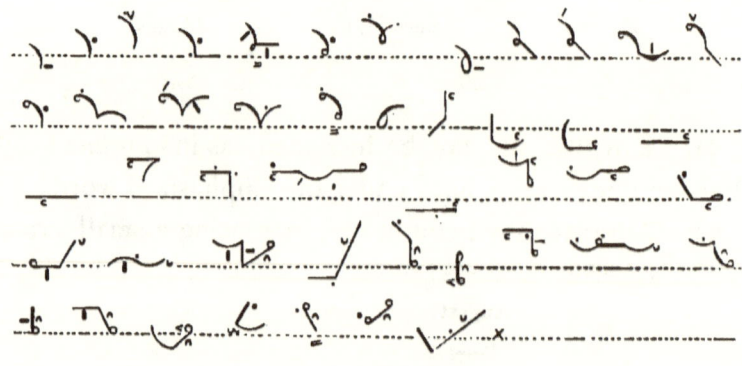

WRITING EXERCISE.

Woe, weigh, awaits, awhile, west, whist, wooes, wheeze, wist, swab, swap, swath, yaw, oyez, yeast, yester-eve, yesterday, quail, squeal, bewail, twitch, twists, equipage, equipoise, bilious, superior, odium, maniac, ague, nephew, argue.

QUESTIONS—LESSON No. 9.

1. How many rules are there for the use of the *w* stroke?   2.   Give them, with an illustration of each rule.   3.   Give the sound represented by *brief W* in the place of *a*.   4.   Give the rules for the use of the *y* stroke.   5.   If the vowel following the brief *W* is a dash vowel, which should be used, *Weh* or *Wuh*?   6.   When is the brief *W* disjoined, used?   7.   Brief *Y* may also be used to represent what?   8.   How may an accented vowel be denoted?   9.   What marks are used for the period?   10.   How is the dash made?

Lesson No. 10.

L HOOK.

93. A small initial hook on the *upper* side of *k* and *g*, and the right side of any *downward straight line* adds *l;* thus,

kl	gl	pl	bl	tl	dl	chl	jl

1. A *small initial* hook on the *concave* side of *f, v, th, sh,* and *zh* adds *l;* thus,

fl	vl	thl	shl	zhl

2. A *large initial* hook on *m, n,* and *Ray* adds *l.* The hook should be about one-half the length of the consonant stroke; thus,

ml	nl	rl

THREE THINGS TO REMEMBER ABOUT THE L HOOK.

94. 1. That it is always at the *beginning* of a consonant stroke.

2. That it is on the *right* side of downward straight lines and the *upper* side of k and g.

3. That it must be made large on m, n, and *Ray*, to be distinct from the W hook on the same letters.

R HOOK.

95. A *small initial* hook on the *lower* side of k and g, and the left side of any *downward straight line* adds r; thus,

kr	gr	pr	br	tr	dr	chr	jr

1. A *small initial* hook on an inverted f, v, or *th* adds r; thus,

fr	vr	thr

The above characters cannot be confused with *Ar*, w, s, or z, because these strokes never take an *initial* hook.

A *small initial* hook on a *shaded m* or n adds r; thus,

mr	nr	rumor	dinner

A *small* hook at the *top* of *sh* and *zh* adds r; thus,

shr	zhr	shriek	measure

50

GENERAL USE OF L AND R HOOKS.

96. The *L* and *R* hooks are used principally when no vowel—or but a slightly sounded one—would occur between the consonant and hook ; as in

| play | blame | broom | payable | final |

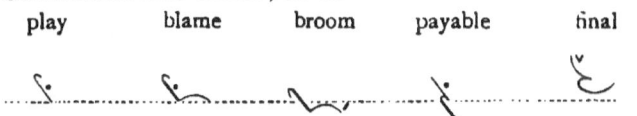

97. VOCALIZATION. A consonant with an *L* or *R* hook is vocalized the same as a simple consonant sign, but the hook must be read *after* the stroke. See examples above.

IMPERFECT HOOKS.

98. It is not always possible to make a perfect hook *between* strokes, but a slight retracing of the preceding consonant will indicate the hook ; thus,

| chipper | dimmer | ripple | gable | baker |

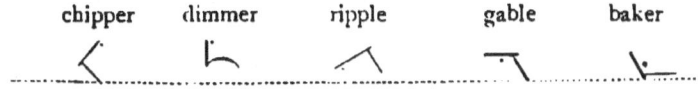

CAUTION.

99. The *R* hook on *m* and *n* must be made small, and the *m* and *n* *shaded*, or confusion will result with the *W* and *L* hooks on the same letters. Note difference :

| nr | mr | wn | wm | nl | ml |

100. Remember that *shl* and *zhl* have their hooks at the *bottom*, and are always written *upward*. *Shr* and *zhr* have their hooks at the top, and are always written *downward*.

101. When *sh* and *l* are the only sounded consonants in a word, the stroke for *l* is generally preferable to the hook.

102. In speaking of the hooked consonants, always call them by name. The name may be ascertained by sounding the vowel ĕ (eh) between the letters represented by the consonant and hook ; thus,

| Pĕl | Mĕr | Nĕl | Rĕl | Chĕl | Wĕr | Shĕr | Fĕr |

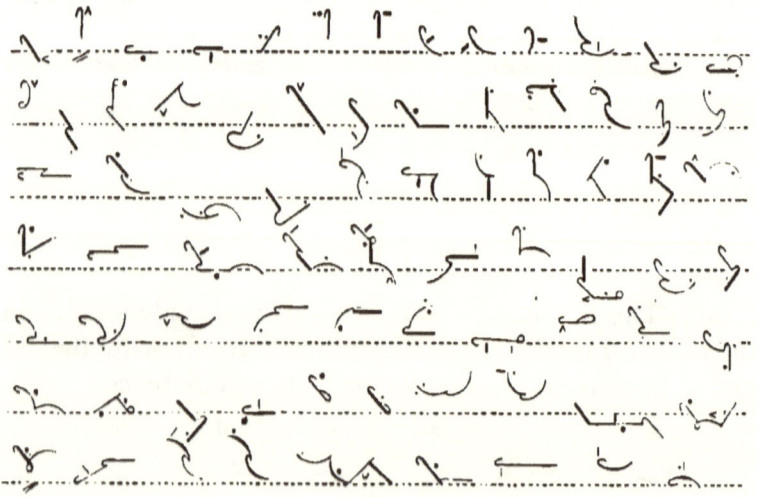

READING EXERCISE.

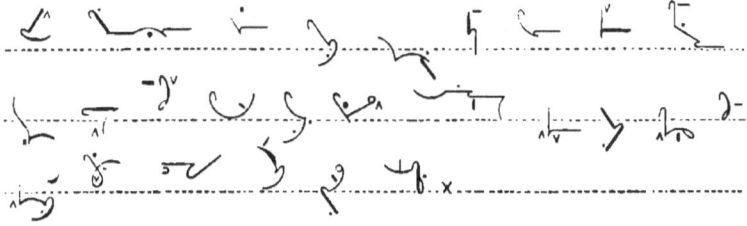

WRITING EXERCISE.

Shriek, crawl, cream, breeder, teacher, decry, trigger, truck, dinner, trifle, buckle, cluster, rimmer, legally, bookmaker, bevel, shaker, drier, maker, clatter, bleacher, author, thrust, glazes, appraise, glossy, fluid, knocker, kennel, crush, freely, eagerly, thickly, trash, jobber, animal, measures, feathery, broker, fly-wheel, peddle, freshly, freer, thrash, throb, deathly, oblige, drawer, precise, swagger, slipper, smuggle, stunner, stumble, blacker, flashily, loafer, flesh, drummer, camel, final, outfly, pepper, neuralgia, philosophy, thrasher, spinner, bleacher, bramble, nimble, tremble, broader, funnel, clams, joggle, thrush, reclaim, swaddle, switcher, replace, rubbers, cooperage, bluster, fluster, shrug, thresh, closed, glazed, classed, oppressed, depressed, propose.

QUESTIONS—LESSON No. 10.

1. A small initial hook on the upper side of *k* and *g* stands for what? 2. What is meant by an initial hook? 3. A small initial hook on the right side of downward straight lines represents what? 4. *L* may be added by a hook to what curve-consonants? 5. What is the difference between *Mẽr* and *Mẽl*? 6. How many initial hooks have *n* and *m*? 7. What is the general rule for the use of the *L* and *R* hooks? 8. What is said about imperfect hooks? 9. Explain the difference between *Shẽr* and *Shẽl*. 10. Can an *L* or *R* hook be read before the consonant to which it is attached?

Lesson No. 11.

SPECIAL USE OF L AND R HOOKS.

103. Long and inconvenient outlines may frequently be avoided by the use of *L* and *R* hooks, even when there is a distinct vowel sound between the *l* or *r* and the preceding consonant, as in *germ, recourse,* etc.

104. VOCALIZATION. In placing a vowel that is to be read *between* a consonant stroke and an *L* or *R* hook, observe the following:

1. Dots are made into circles and written *before* the stroke if the vowel is long ; *after,* if short; thus,

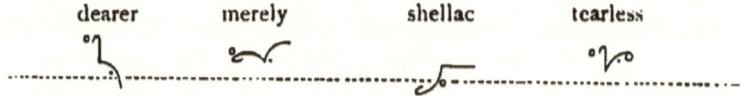

| dearer | merely | shellac | tearless |

When the above rule would bring the circle into an angle, as in *shark,* it should be disregarded and the circle written in the most convenient manner.

2. Dashes are struck through the stroke; thus,

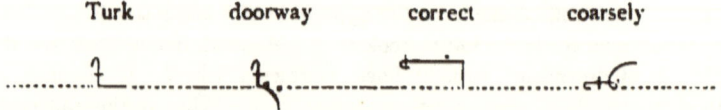

| Turk | doorway | correct | coarsely |

3. Diphthongs and semi-circles may be struck through, or written at the beginning or end of the stroke ; thus,

qualify   procure   figures

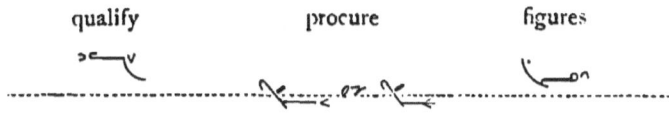

ISS PREFIXED TO AN L HOOK.

105. *Iss* may be joined to an *L* hook by a slightly flattened circle written within the hook ; thus,

supply   civil   briskly   disclaim   gospel

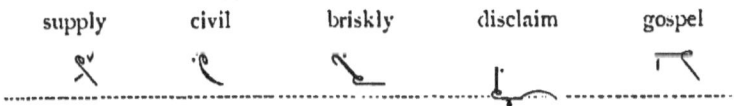

CAUTION. Neither the large circle, nor the *Steh* or *Ster loop* is prefixed to the *L hook*.

ISS, SEZ, AND STEH PREFIXED TO R HOOKS.

106. Writing a small circle in place of the *R* hook on *straight* lines prefixes *s;* a large circle, *s-s;* thus,

straw   seeker   suppress   sister

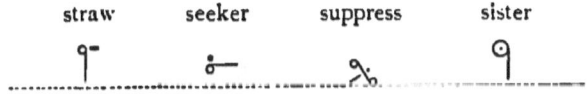

2. Writing a small loop in place of the hook prefixes *st.*

stutter   stupor   steeper   stitcher

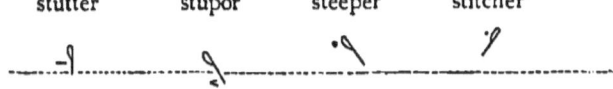

CAUTION.   The *Ster loop* is never prefixed to an *R* hook.

2.   Between *p, b, t, d, ch, j,* and *kr* and *gr, s* is added by making the circle on the right side of *p, b,* etc., and joining the *k* or *g* from the *top* of the circle; also between *ch, j,* and *pr* or *br,* by joining *p* or *b* in the same manner.

| superscribe | disgrace | subscriber | Jasper |

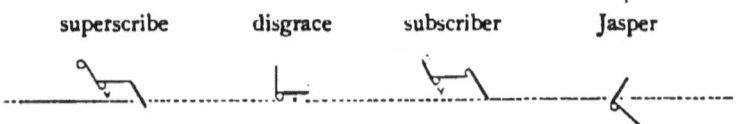

4.   *Iss* or *Sez* may be prefixed to the *R* hook, between two straight lines *in the same direction,* by turning the circle on the lower side of *k* or *g,* and on the left side of any other stroke; thus,

| execrable | prosper | disaster | destroy | Boasberg |

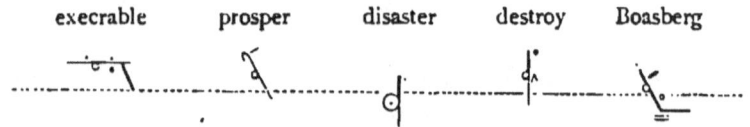

5.   In other cases the circle is prefixed by writing it distinctly within the hook; thus,

| extra | passover | designer | listener |

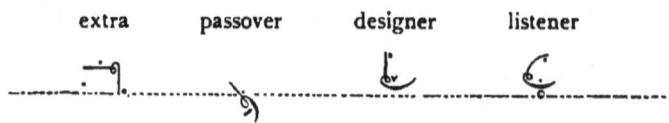

107.   Of the curved *R* hook-signs, *n* is the only one taking *initial Iss;* hence, the *r* in such words as *summer, suffer,* etc., should be expressed by a stroke, not with a hook.

| sinner | sooner | summer | suffer |

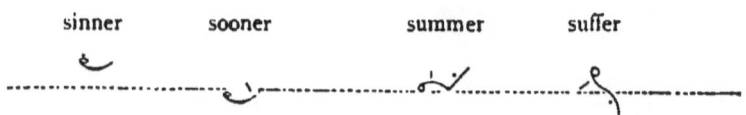

108. NAMES *Per, Bel, Kel, Ter, Ner,* etc., with *Iss* prefixed should be called

Iss-Per	Iss-Pel	Iss-Kel	Iss-Ter	Iss-Ner, etc.

If more convenient, and the syllable can be easily spoken, they may be called *Sper, Spel, Skel,* etc.

READING EXERCISE.

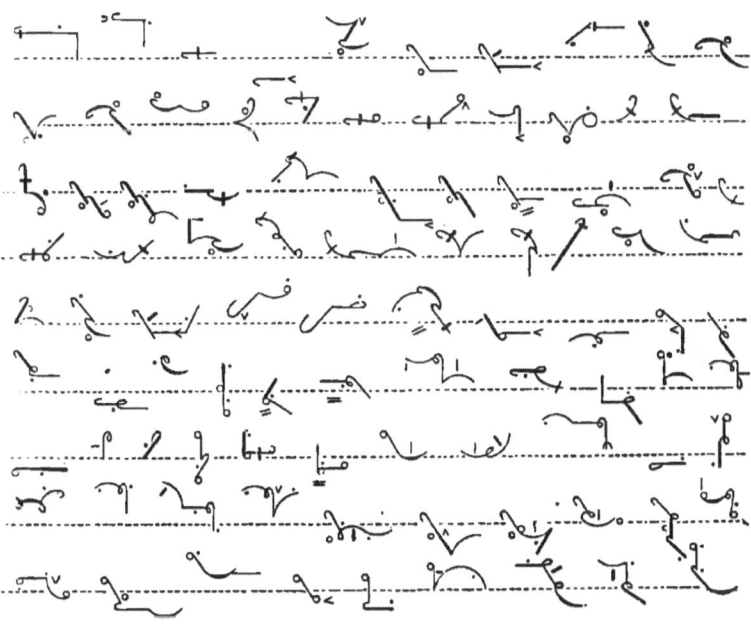

WRITING EXERCISE.

Turk, coal-black, coarsely, burst, charm, foolscap, occurs, shark, shares, gore, careless, church, apple-tree, portray, sea·shore, filigree, filthy, fork, firmly, film, forsake, forkless, term, car, curb, chirp, pearl, carboy, appear, sharp, pioneer, courage, foolish, slavery, skirmish, endures, ungear, verily, torch, qualify, unfurl, curable, paralyze, sobriety, smoker, soaker, sunstruck, supplies, suppressor, superinduce, traceable, taxidermist, speaker, secrecy, strainer, stopper, stripper, outstretch, pasture, moisture, settle, descry, discourage, suitor, feasible, scare, depositor, distressed, supervisal, disagreeable, blissful, scrabble.

QUESTIONS—LESSON No. 11.

1. How should a dot vowel be written so as to be read between a stroke and hook? 2. When ā is to be read between a stroke and hook, where do you place it? 3. How do you indicate that ŏ is to be read between a stroke and hook? 4. How must diphthongs and semi-circles be written so as to be read between the hook and stroke? 5. How is *Iss* prefixed to an initial *R* hook on straight lines? 6. Is *Iss* prefixed to the *R* hook on *m*, *f*, *v*, and *th* when the hook is initial? 7. How may *Iss* be added to an *L* hook? 8. How may *st* be prefixed to an *R* hook on straight lines? 9. Is the *Ster* loop ever prefixed to a hook? 10. How is *r* represented between *D-Iss* and *K*? 11. How is *Iss* prefixed to an *R* hook between two straight lines in the same direction?

Lesson No. 12.

ENLARGED L AND R HOOKS.

109. *L* may be added to an *R* hook by making the hook twice the usual size.

110. *R* may be added to a *small L* hook by making the hook twice the usual size.

| April | mackerel | abler | dabbler |

111. *S* may be prefixed to an enlarged *L* or *R* hook by writing the circle distinctly within the hook.

112. When a vowel is placed after a consonant stroke with an enlarged hook, it is read *between* the *l* and *r*. See *April* and *abler* in preceding illustration.

113 *P*, with an enlarged *R* hook, may be called *Prel;* with an enlarged *L* hook, *Pler:* *K* with an enlarged *L* hook, *Kler;* with an enlarged *R* hook, *Krel;* etc., etc. If the circle is prefixed, then, *Iss-Prel, Iss-Pler*, etc.

IN, UN, OR EN.

114. The initial syllable, *in, un,* or *en*, when followed by *Iss*, may be prefixed by a *curved hook*, called the *In* hook.

1. To any straight line *R* hook-sign; occasionally to an *L* hook-sign ; thus,

unstring   ensober   uncivilized   unsettle

2. To any other consonant, to avoid turning the circle on the back of *N;* thus,

unsullied   unseemly   unsurmised

READING EXERCISE.

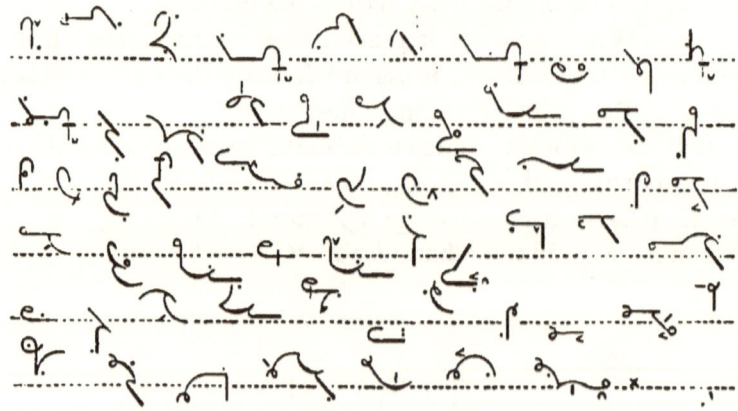

WRITING EXERCISE.

Pickerel, temporal, lustral, timbrel, Charles, gambler, clearness, colorless, smuggler, stickler, clerical, saddler, clergy, nibbler, ocular, buckler, straggler, cobbler, tippler, tattler, implore, flourish, giggler, glare, implorer, jocular, jumbler, spicular, mangler, leveler, simpler, scribbler, un-struck, unsociable, insecurely, enslave, enscroll, insuper-able, unswung, enslaver.

WORD SIGNS—CONTRACTIONS.

⌐ . . . . . till, tell, it will	. . . . . every, very
⌐ . . . . until, at all	through
⌐ . . . . . call, equally	. their, there, they are
⌐ . . . . . . difficult-y	other
⌐ . . . . full, fully	sure, surely
⌐ . . . . value	pleasure
⌐ . . . principle, principal	Mr., mere, remark
⌐ . . . . surprise	more
⌐ . . . member, remember	near, nor
⌐ . . . . number-ed	manner
⌐ . . . . dear	Mrs.
⌐ . . . . truth	Messrs.
⌐ . . . . during	capable

```
...⌐⌐...  . . . . . . . care          ⌐ .  . . . . . . influential

...⌐...... . . . . . . . from          ⌐\ . . . . . . . . proper

...⌐\_ . . . . . . . . . over          ...\... . . . . . . . capability

⌐o-- . . . . . . transgress          \⌐ . . . . probable-ility
```

QUESTIONS—LESSON No. 12.

1. Enlarging an *R* hook adds what? 2. Enlarging a small *L* hook adds what? 3. How may *Iss* be prefixed to an enlarged *L* or *R* hook? 4. When a vowel is placed after a consonant with an enlarged hook, where is it read? 5. What name would you give to *t*, *d*, *k*, *g*, with an enlarged *L* hook? 6. Write *Iss-Kler*, *Iss-Bler*, *Iss-Brel*, and *Iss-Nerl*. 7. How may initial *In*, *un*, or *en* be represented? 8. To what may the *In*, *Un*, and *En* hooks be joined? 9. What name is given to these hooks?

Lesson No. 13.

FINAL HOOKS FOR F, V, AND N.

115. A small hook at the end, and on the circle side of any straight line consonant, adds *f* or *v;* thus,

puff	cover	rave	huff	chief

With the aid of the context, and a little practice, no confusion will result from employing the same hook for *f* and *v*.

116. A small hook at the end of any straight line consonant, and *opposite* the circle side, adds *n;* thus,

den	cleaner	ran	gun	chin

This will bring the *N* hook on the *under* side of *k*, *g*, *Ray*, and *h*, and on the *left* side of all other straight strokes.

117. *N* may also be added to any curve by a small final hook on the inner, or concave side; thus,

fine	vainer	minute	Orrin	assign

118. The *F* or *V* hook is rarely added to a curve sign, and then, usually, to denote the addition of *have*.

119. VOCALIZATION. A vowel placed after a stroke with an *F*, *V*, or *N* hook, must be read *between* the stroke and the hook. In other words, the hook must be read *after* any vowel placed beside the stroke. See preceding illustration.

120. USE THE STROKE for *f*, *v*, or *n* whenever these letters precede a *final* vowel, as in

coffee	purify ˙	funny	bevy

ALSO when *f*, *v*, or *n* precedes a vowel and final *s*, as in

diffuse	profuse ˙	revise	denies

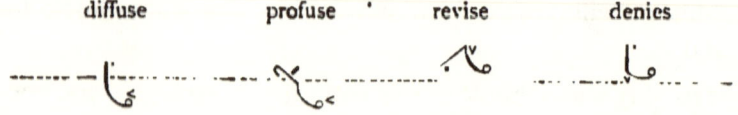

CIRCLES AND LOOPS ADDED TO FINAL HOOKS.

121. *S* may be added to the *F* and *V* hooks, and to the *N* hook on curves, by writing the small circle distinctly within the hooks; thus,

raves	puffs	means	fans	thins

122. *S*, *s-s*, *st*, or *str* may be added to the *N* hook on any *straight* line, by writing their respective signs in place of the hook; thus,

pens	Kansas	chanced	spinster	glanced

123. The loops and the large circle are never added to the *F* or *V* hooks. CAUTION. The loops and large circle are never added to the *N* hook *between strokes*.

The small circle may be added. but only when it can be distinctly written within the hook; thus,

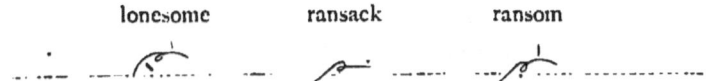

lonesome   ransack   ransom

124. When the *w* stroke takes a final hook it should be called *Way;* thus. *Iss-Wayn* or *Swayn* is the name of the outline for *Swoon.*

READING EXERCISE.

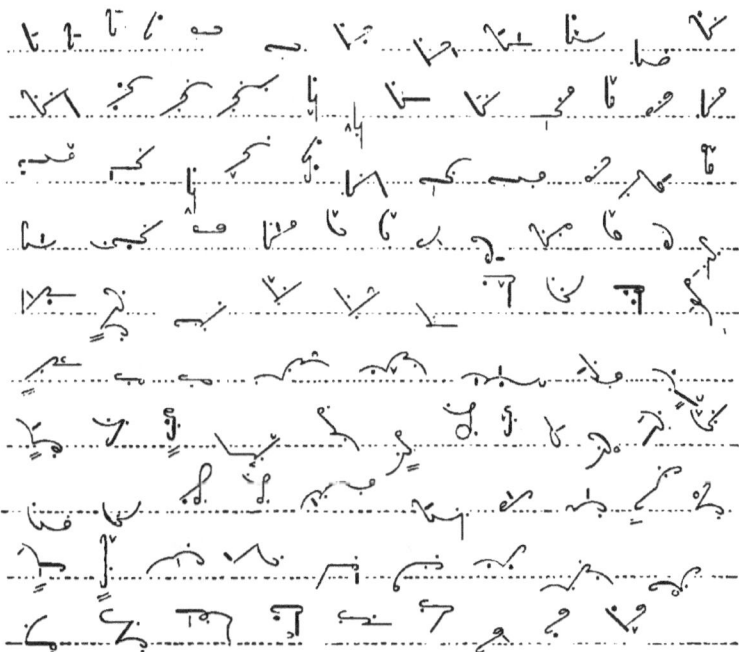

WRITING EXERCISE.

Gave, rave, roof, staffs, braver, cough, rebuffs, call, siphon, heaves, cloves, roofless, divers, cleaver, edified, devoid, devote, graver, engraves, reverse, drives, endeavors, beverage, gloves, retrieves, bee-hives, prefers, preferences, rougher, typhoon, fan, mine, cone, ran, span, doorman, wooden, urn, swan, economy, vainer, cleanly, brownish, vacancy, piquancy, dens, dances, danced, punish, French, quinsy, gleans, Spencer, shines, ozone, tenth, thrones, pancake, thinish, spinsters, bobbins, frowns, liken, knee-pan, kinsman, cancer, sustain, swollen, trepan, turban, unclean, uncrown, undriven, unanimous, volcanic, warn, yarn, sevens, profane, furnish, ferns, adjourn, advances, serenely, stanza, expanse, tenses, prance, trances, ingrain, wagons, melons, Lancaster, mechanic, enthrone, enlivens, silken, moonshine, appertain, oceans, lemonade, moss-grown, monopoly, sweeten, bounced.

QUESTIONS—LESSON No. 13.

1. What does a small hook at the end, and on the circle side of a straight-line consonant represent? 2. A small hook on straight lines, and opposite the circle side represents what? 3. A small hook at the end of curves represents what? 4. A vowel placed after a stroke having an *F*, *V*, or *N* hook is read where? 5. When must the stroke for *f*, *v*, or *n* be used? 6. How may the small circle be added to the *F*, *V*, and *N* hooks? 7. How is final *lss* added to an *N* hook on a straight line? 8. How is *Sez* added? 9. How are *st* and *str* added? 10. Are the loops and large circle ever added to the *F* or *V* hooks? 11. What is said about the addition of a small circle to the *N* hook between strokes?

Lesson No. 14.

SYLLABLES, SHON AND TIV.

125. SHON—This syllable, (spelled, *tion, cion, cian, sion,* etc., in different words) may be added to any consonant by a *large* final hook, written on the circle side of straight strokes, and the inner, or concave side of curved strokes ; thus,

motion	coercion	magician	diffusion	visionary

126. *Tiv, added to straight lines only,* is indicated by a large hook, written opposite the circle side; thus,

active	defectiveness	dative	collective

127. The small circle may be written within the *Shon* and *Tiv* hooks to add *s.*

SMALL HOOK FOR SHON—CALLED ESHON.

128. When the sound of *shon* is preceded by *a vowel and s*, it is usually best represented by a small hook added to the *Iss* circle ; thus,

physician	transition	transitional	suppositions	succession

129. VOCALIZATION. Vowels occurring between the *s* and *shon* may be written at the left of the hook, if first place, and at the right, if second or third place. It is rarely necessary, however, to vocalize an *Eshon* hook.

130. The small circle may be written inside the *Eshon* hook to add a final *s*. See *suppositions* in preceding illustration.

READING EXERCISE.

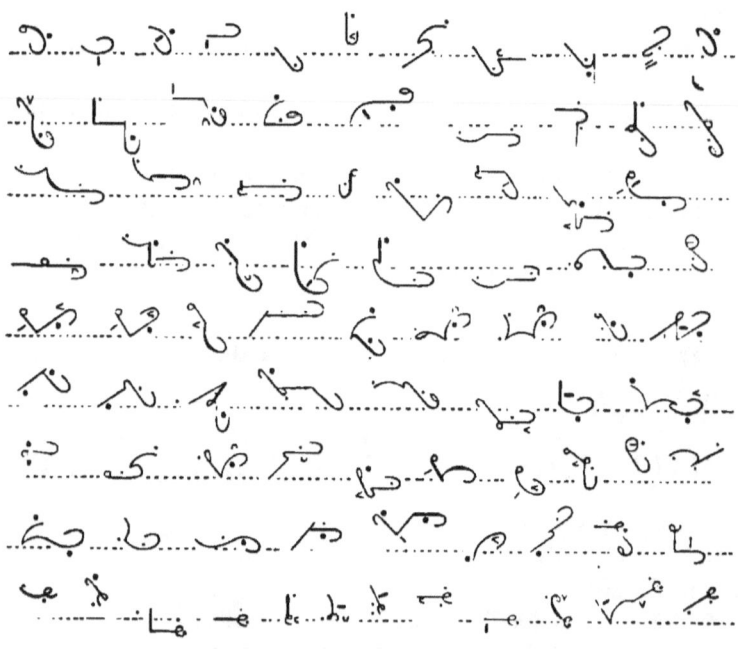

WRITING EXERCISE.

Logician, ineffective, remission, rotation, delusion, restorative, Russian, ruination, submission, incarceration, inattention, auction, attraction, negative, division, perfective, radiation, deception, regulation, palliation, vocation, version, abrasion, assertion, eruption, irrigation, immersion, inspiration, illustration, perception, activeness, professional, receptive, suppression, instruction, duration, mansions, revisions, extermination, prosecution, deprivation, fermentation, desolation, desecration, additional, electioneer, ignition, sub-section, seclusion, population, friction, veneration, captivity, restorative, distillation, cineration, collisions, execution, opposition, persuasion, procession, acquisition, perquisition, moralization, indecision, imprecision, disquisition, authorization, relaxation, disposition, deposition, dispossession, dispensation, depreciation, crystallization.

--

QUESTIONS—LESSON No. 14.

1. A large hook at the end of any curve consonant represents what ? 2. What does it represent on the circle side of straight lines? 3. A large final hook on straight strokes, and opposite the circle side, represents what ? 4. Is the *Tiv* hook added to curves? 5. How may *s* be added to the *Shon* and *Tiv* hooks ? 6. What is the *Eshon* hook ? 7. When is the *Eshon* hook usually employed ? 8. If a vowel occur between the *s* and *shon*, where should it be placed ? 9. May the small circle be added to the *Eshon* hook ?

Lesson No. 15.

M SHADED TO ADD P OR B.

131.　*M* may be shaded to add *p* or *b*; thus,

imp	ambition	bump	stamp	impose

132.　Shaded *m* is called *Emp* when *p* is added, and *Emb* when *b* is added.

133.　*Emp* and *Emb* never take an *initial* hook, though a *final* hook may be added.

134.　*P* may be omitted when it occurs between *m* and *Shon*, in such words as,

presumption	assumption	pre-emption

LENGTHENED STROKES.

135.　Double the length

1.　Of *Emp* or *Emb* to add *er*; thus,

romper	timber	jumpers

2. Of *Ing* to add *kr* to *gr;* thus,

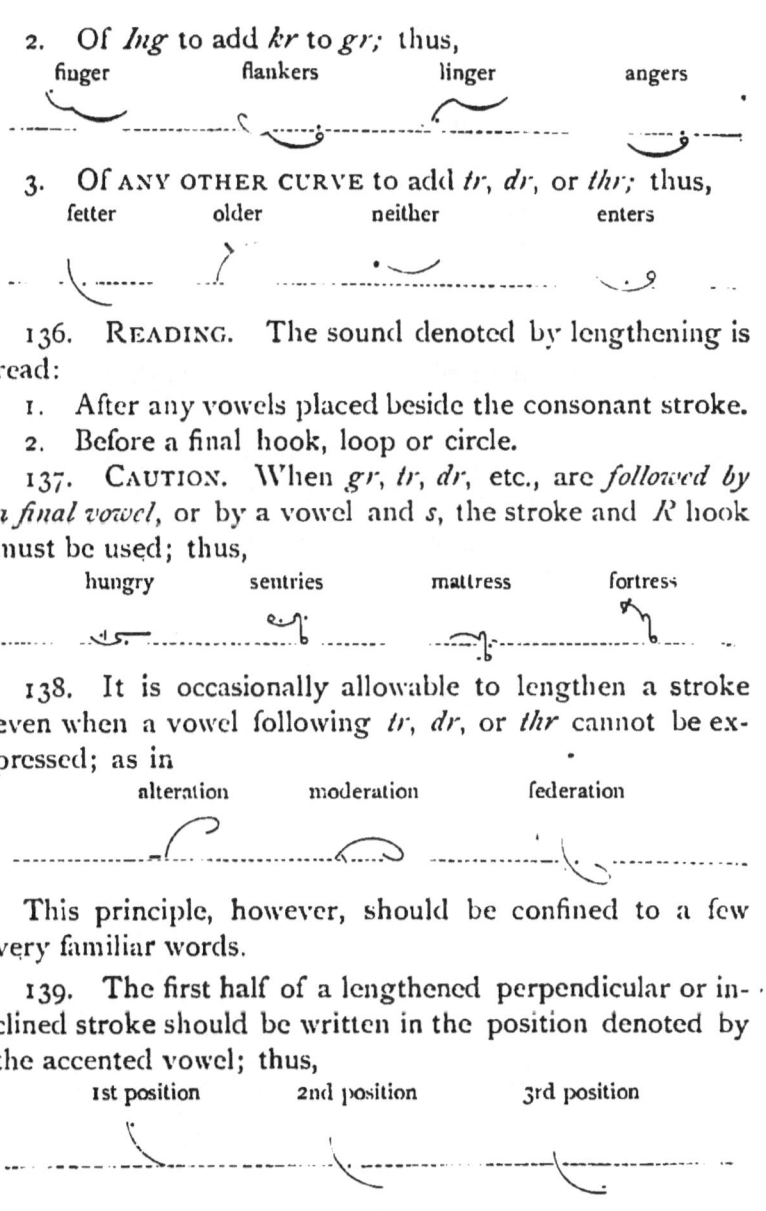

finger   flankers   linger   angers

3. Of ANY OTHER CURVE to add *tr*, *dr*, or *thr;* thus,

fetter   older   neither   enters

136. READING. The sound denoted by lengthening is read:

1. After any vowels placed beside the consonant stroke.

2. Before a final hook, loop or circle.

137. CAUTION. When *gr*, *tr*, *dr*, etc., are *followed by a final vowel*, or by a vowel and *s*, the stroke and *R* hook must be used; thus,

hungry   sentries   mattress   fortress

138. It is occasionally allowable to lengthen a stroke even when a vowel following *tr*, *dr*, or *thr* cannot be expressed; as in

alteration   moderation   federation

This principle, however, should be confined to a few very familiar words.

139. The first half of a lengthened perpendicular or inclined stroke should be written in the position denoted by the accented vowel; thus,

1st position   2nd position   3rd position

THERE, THEIR, THEY ARE, OR OTHER.

140. Any *curve* or *straight* line, without a final hook, loop, or circle, may be lengthened to add *thr* for *there*, *their*, *they are*, or *other;* thus,

in *their*   by *their*
in *there*   by *there*   check *their*   among *their*
in *other*   by *other*   among *other*

The context will readily indicate which word, or words are added.

141. Straight lines may occasionally be lengthened to add *tr*, *dr*, or *thr*, as in *quarter*, *conductor*, *rather*, etc.

This principle is rarely used when the consonant is initial.

NAMES. The lengthened strokes are called *Ember*, *Ingger*, *Layter*, etc.; the name of the consonant being prefixed to that of the added syllable.

READING EXERCISE.

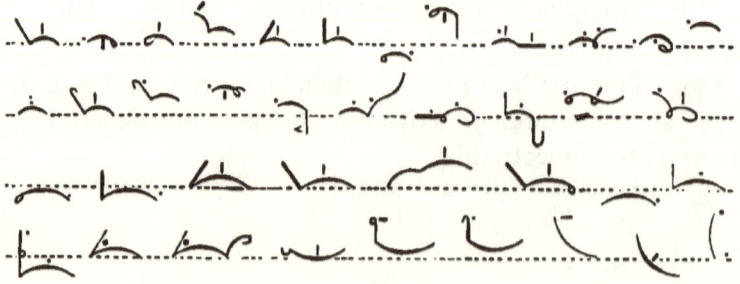

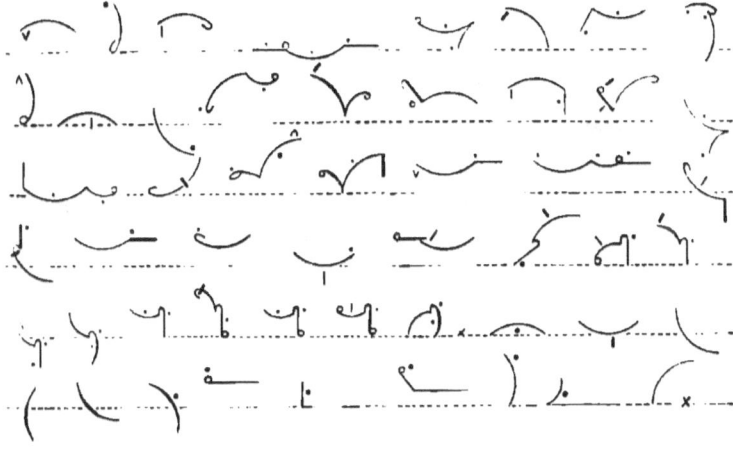

WRITING EXERCISE.

Damp, vamp, impute, ambitious, impede, clamp, shampoo, shrimp, trump, cramp, imbues, embody, camp, clump, pomp, tramp, impish, mump, emperor, empty, redemption.

Simper, limber, hamper, plumper, cumber, stamper, amber-seed, clamber, cumbersome, pamper, somber, whimper, somberly, tramper, hanker, monger, languor, fingerless, canker, sinkers, clinkers, anchorless, franker, smother, render, slender, disorder, flutter, literary, fender, banter, loiters, water, diameter, swelter, motherless, fatherless, wanderer, Arthur, smoother, engender, wilder, molder, dissenter, defender, metrical, nitrate, orderly, promoter, recounter, shatter, shelter, slaughter-house, smother, stockholder, surrender, waterproof, wintry, Andrew, angry, artery, paltry, laundry, propagator, squatter, supporter, wood-cutter, spectre, speculator.

In their, wish their, own their, while there, why they are, over their, whenever they are, in other, one other, black their, beg their, wreak their.

To save useless repetition, *thr* is used to represent there, their, they are, or other.

From thr, whenever thr, in thr, do thr, know thr, was thr, use thr, hear thr, value thr, may thr, shake thr, through thr, fling thr, lay thr, when thr, why thr, have thr, own thr.

WORD SIGNS—CONTRACTIONS.

Sign	Word	Sign	Word
	above		opinion
	again		objection
	another		objective
	before		often, phonograph-y
	been		phonographer
	can		phonographic
	careful-ly		remembrance
	different-ly		representation
	entire		representative
	farther, further		subjection
	general-ly		subjective
	important-ce		truthful-ly

...⌒... . .improve-ment, may be   .....⌐... . . . . upon

...⌐⌐... . . . . impossible-ility   ....⌐... . . . .`. whatever

...⌐... . . . . . investigation   ...⌐... . . . . . . whichever

...⌐... . . . . men   ....⌐... . . . . . . .who have

...⌐... . . . . man   (within

QUESTIONS—LESSON No. 15.

1. *M* may be shaded to add what? 2. Does *Emp* or *Emb* ever take an initial hook? 3. Do they take the final hooks, loops and circles? 4. Doubling the length of *Emp* or *Emb* adds what? 5. Doubling the length of *Ing* adds what? 6. Doubling the length of any other curve adds what? 7. Is the sound denoted by lengthening read before or after a final hook, loop or circle? 8. Can the lengthening principle be employed where the *tr*, *dr*, etc., precede a final vowel? 9. What is said about the position of a lengthened stroke? 10. May straight lines be lengthened? 11. What is said about the lengthening of initial straight lines? 12. How may *there*, *they are*, or *other* be added to a full length stroke without a final hook, loop or circle?

Lesson No. 16.

SHORTENED LETTERS.

142.   *T* or *d* may be added to any consonant stroke, except *w* and *y*, by making it half its usual length; thus,

pet	spade	.	spent	plants	refined

The context will enable one to determine whether *t* or *d* is added.

143.   METHOD OF READING.   The *t* or *d* denoted by shortening, must be read *after* a final hook, but *before* a final circle; thus,

band	tufts	bands	rents	heft

144.   *Emp* and *Emb* are halved only when they take a final hook.

145.   Shortened *El*, *m*, *n*, and *Ar* are generally shaded when *d* is added; thus,

old	mode	need	hard	snowed

146. *Wem* or *Wen* must not be shaded when shortened, as they would conflict with shortened *Mer* and *Ner*.

147. A shortened *s* may sometimes be written upward to advantage when joined to an *N* or *Shon* hook, as in,

    fashionist   factionist   canonist, etc.

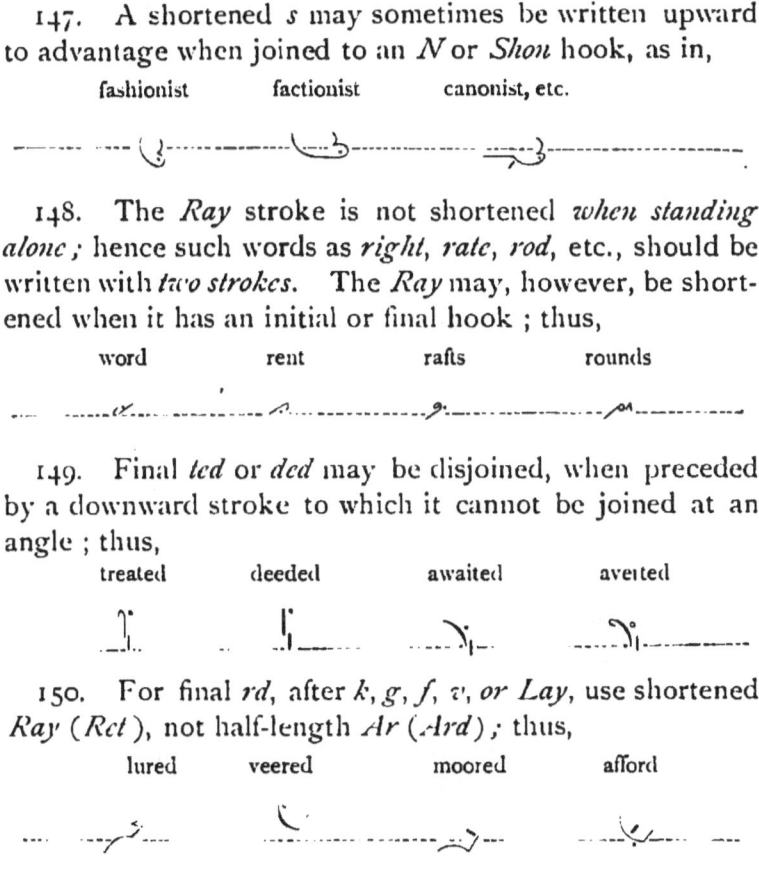

148. The *Ray* stroke is not shortened *when standing alone;* hence such words as *right, rate, rod,* etc., should be written with *two strokes.* The *Ray* may, however, be shortened when it has an initial or final hook ; thus,

    word   rent   rafts   rounds

149. Final *ted* or *ded* may be disjoined, when preceded by a downward stroke to which it cannot be joined at an angle ; thus,

    treated   deeded   awaited   averted

150. For final *rd,* after *k, g, f, v, or Lay,* use shortened *Ray* (*Ret*), not half-length *Ar* (*Ard*); thus,

    lured   veered   moored   afford

WHEN NOT TO SHORTEN.

151. The halving principle should not be used in the following cases :

1. When the junction would not indicate the addition of a shortened letter, as in

| looked | effect | minute | fatigue |

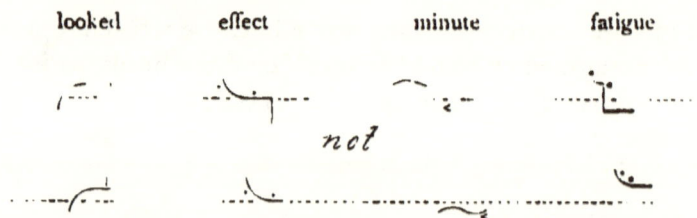

not

2. When the *t* or *d* is followed by a final vowel, or by a vowel and a final *Iss*, as in

| windy | naughty | Sundays |

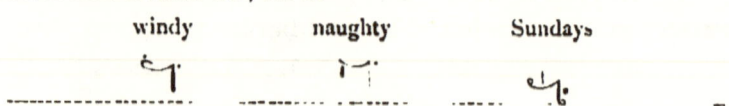

NOTE. The object of the above rule is to make a distinction between monosyllables and words of two syllables; as *wind*, *windy*; *naught*, *naughty*; *winds*, *windows*.

3. When an initial vowel is followed by a consonant and a vowel, which immediately precede final *t* or *d*; as in

| afoot | avowed | abed |

NOTE The object of the above rule is to make a distinction between such words as *foot*, *afoot*; *vowed*, *avowed*; *bed*, *abed*.

4. When two vowels immediately precede the *t* or *d*; as in

| Druid | fluid | quiet | Hyatt |

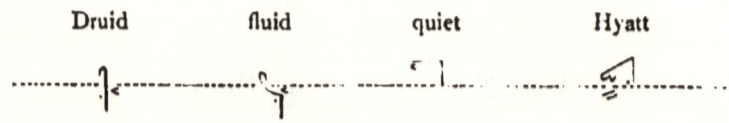

NOTE. The object of the above rule is to make a distinction between such words as *quite* and *quiet*; *Jute* and *Jewett*.

5. When *l*, *r*, or *n* is preceded by a vowel and a consonant, and followed by a sounded vowel and final *d* (*not t*); as in

mellowed	married	renewed	flurried

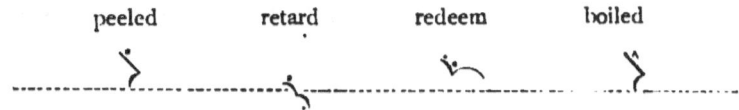

Note 1. The object of the above rule is to make a distinction between such words as *marred* and *married; ruined* and *renewed*.

Note 2. If the vowels were always inserted there would be little need of the foregoing rules; but as the advanced phonographer does not write one vowel in a hundred, such distinction becomes necessary to the easy and accurate reading of shorthand notes.

Names. The shortened letters may be called *Bet, Ret, Chet, Met,* etc. When *d* is added, they may (if preferred) be called *Bed, Red, Ched, Med,* etc. Shortened *L, Ar,* and *Ish* are named *Let* or *Eld, Art* or *Ard,* and *Isht* or *Shet.*

152. For the sake of speed and legibility, the rules governing the use of *R* and *L* are sometimes disregarded when these letters are shortened; thus,

peeled	retard	redeem	boiled

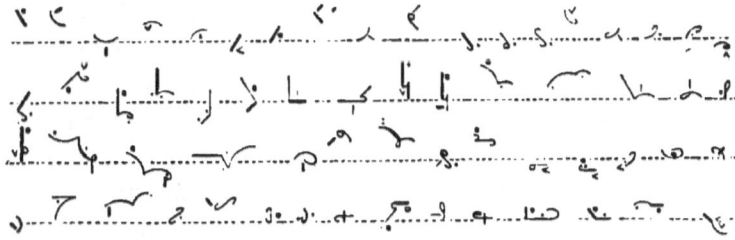

READING EXERCISE.

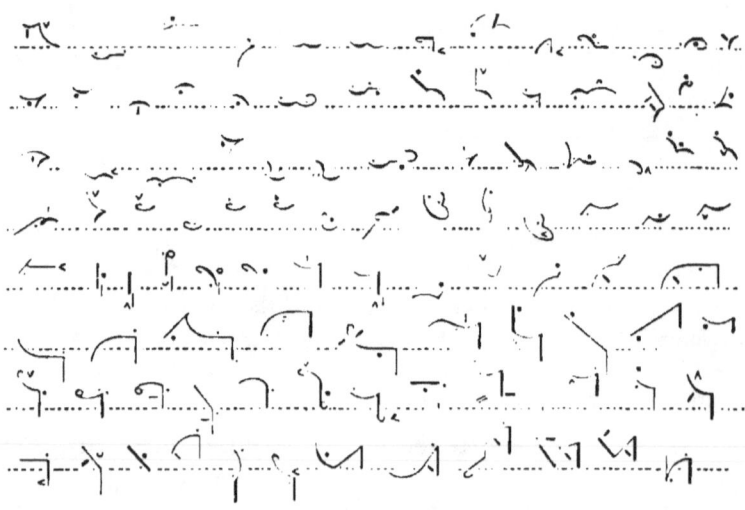

WRITING EXERCISE.

Pad, boot, taught, dude, chide, dot, jot, caught, cute, foot, void, thought, eased, shod, light, hired, hunt, bound, spent, saddened, stunned, fanned, funds, paved, breathed, divested, patched, muzzled, defeated, islands, bumped, studied, rounds, fashioned, stride, stained, moment, potato, drowned, secrete, staggered, fitly, lived, skilled, roiled, lightness, coiled, glands, rants, protection, dedicate, bottom, indisposition, indigent, illegitimate (El jet-met), modify, meditate, plenitude, antedate, abdicate, obdurate, agitated, pottage, bitter, graduation, avidity, metal, indicated, ultimate, sold, plumed, bored, reasoned, barred, defined, tarred, scared, deemed, growled, curtailed, hardened, peeled, hard, loomed, resigned, descend, factionist, elocutionist, windward, twined, wand, vainest, excursionist, rowed, reed, route, ward, wired, round, rents, antedated, strutted, retreated, defrauded, inverted, amputated, undated, treated, mired, mart, suffered, slurred, immured,

leered, fortified, forgot, (1) slacked, liked, flecked, evict,
collect, clicked, cracked, crocked, gagged, bobbed, roared,
(2) body, Betty, fatty, giddy, Cato, lady, motto, ruddy,
shady, lotus, lattice, meadows, veto, (3) allude, edit, assayed,
aside, allied, elate, omit, equate, (4) riot, albeit, Piatt,
(5) buried, denied, dallied, ferried, torrid, sallied, solid,
carried, hurried, horrid, rallied.

WORD SIGNS AND CONTRACTIONS.

. . . . about	immediate-ly	. . . . put
. . . account	. inconsistent	. . somewhat
acknowledged	indiscriminate	. . . spirit
. according-ly	indispensable	. . . . . that
. . . . after	. . in order	. . . . till it
. . afterward	. intelligible	. . . . told
astonish-ed-ment	. intelligence	. . . toward
. . . could	. . intelligent	. . throughout
establish-ed-ment	. . . interest	. . transcript
. . . forward	. . it will not	. . we are not
. . gentlemen	. . Lord, read	. . . were not
. . gentleman	. . . . nature	. . . will not
. . . . good	. . natural-ly	. . without
. . . . heard	. opportunity	. . . . world
as it, has it, hesitate-d-ion hundred-th, under	. particular-ly	
	practicable-ility	

81

153. Derivatives of words represented by word-signs, may be formed by adding to the sign of the primitive the consonant necessary to form the derivative; thus,

value   valued   call   called   world   worldly

154. When a word sign or contraction does not contain the last consonant of the primitive word, the derivative is rarely formed by shortening; hence the signs for *object*, *remark*, etc., should not be shortened for *objected*, *remarked*, etc., but a full length *t* or *d* should be added.

155. Great care should be taken to make the shortened letters only *half* as long as the full length strokes, as otherwise confusion will result.

QUESTIONS—LESSON No. 16.

1. What letters are not shortened? 2. When must the *t* or *d* denoted by halving be read? 3. What is said about halving *Emp* and *Emb?* 4. What letters may be shaded when halved? 5. May shortened *Wem* and *Wen* be shaded? 6. When may shortened *s* be written upward? 7. Is the simple *Ray* stroke ever halved? 8. What is said about disjoining *ted* or *ded?* 9. How should *lard* be written? 10. How should *slacked* be written? 11. What is the object in so writing it? 12. How should *putty* be written? 13. Under what rule does this come? 14. How should *abate* be written? 15. Would *abound* come under the rule that governs the writing of *abed?* 16. What rule would govern the writing of *gayety?*

Lesson No. 17.

BRIEF PREFIX SIGNS.

156. **Con, Com,** or **Cog,** beginning a word, may be represented by a light dot, written before the remainder of the word; thus,

confess · complain   cognizance   content   complex

a. **Con, Com,** or **Cog,** when occurring in the middle of a word, may be omitted and implied by writing the part preceding *Con, Com,* or *Cog, over* or *near* the remainder of the word; thus,

decomposition   discontent   nonconformist   misconstrue

uncompressed   recognized   irreconciliation   inconceivable

1. **Accom,** may be represented by a heavy dot, written before the remainder of the word; thus,

accomplish   accommodation   accompany   accompanist

83

a. **Con, Com, Cog,** or *Accom* may also often be advantageously implied by writing the remainder of the word under a preceding word or stroke; thus,

in the complaint   nice accommodations   will condemn

2. **Contra, Contro, Counter,** may be represented by a tick, written at the beginning of the remainder of the word; thus,

contraband   controvert   countercheck   countermine

3. **Incon** and **Uncom,** when followed by *s*, may sometimes be advantageously represented by the *In* hook; thus,

inconsiderable   in consideration   inconsolable   inconsumable

4. **Inter, Intro** may be represented by *Net*, written before, or joined to the remainder of the word; thus,

intercept   introduction   introduce   interrupt

5. **For** and **Fore** are usually expressed by *f*, joined to or written before the remainder of the word; thus,

forward   forefather   forenoon   foreseen

It is occasionally better to represent these prefixes in such words as *forget, forgive, foremost,* etc, by *Fer* or *F-Ar.*

6. **In=re.** The word *in,* with the following initial syllable, *re,* may often be advantageously represented by *Ner*

joined to the remainder of the word; thus,

in reply	in response	in receipt	in respect

7. **Magne, Magna, Magni** may be expressed by *m*, written over the remainder of the word; thus,

magnesia	magnanimous	magnitude	magnify

8. **Self** is expressed by a small circle, joined to, or written beside the first stroke of the remainder of the word.

a. *Self* may also be joined to a following *Iss* by enlarging the circle.

selfish	self-devoted	self-same	self-sacrifice

b. *Self-con, com, cog* may be expressed by writing the small circle in place of the *con* dot.

c. *Self-contra* may be expressed by joining *self* to the tick for *contra*

9. **Prefixes joined.** Prefix-signs may be joined to initial syllables, and to each other; as in *uncontradicted*, *self-interest*, etc. Word-signs may also be used as prefix signs; as *Fet-Nen* for *afternoon*, *End-Gay* for *undergo*, etc.

READING EXERCISE.

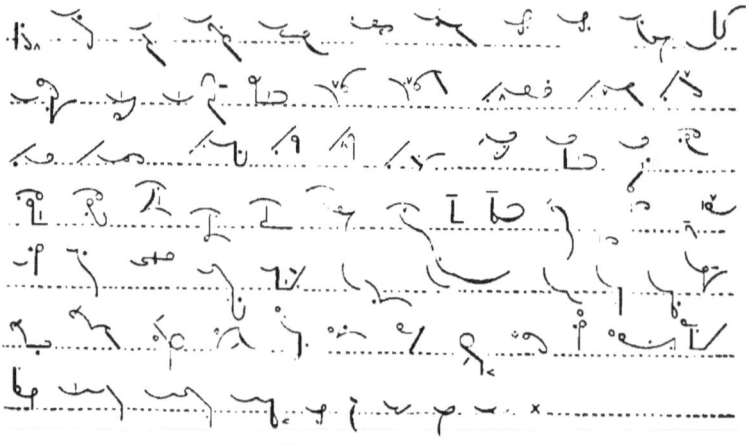

WRITING EXERCISE.

OMIT UNACCENTED VOWELS.

1. Confuse, conceit, commemorate, commend, commit, cognomen, communication, competition, complainer, comrade, conceivable, concoction, concurrent, condescend, confederate, confinement, congratulation, conscript, accompaniment, accomplishment, common, complaint, kind consideration, will commence, will accompany, discomfort, disconnection, discontent, disconsolate, decomposed, disconnected, incomposite, inconsistency, inconsiderately, inconsolably, inconsumably, inconvenience, incomplete, incognito, unconcern, unconditional, uncompromising, uncomfortably, unconstitutional, in receipting, in reducing. irreconcilably, irreconcilement, recognize, recommend, recompile, recommit, reconstruct, recumbency, noncommittal, nonconductor, nonconformity, misconduct, misconstrued, miscompute, magnetic, magnetize, magnanimously,

magnificent, magnify, contradiction, contradictive, contro-
vertible, counter-brace, counterfeit, counterpane, intercept,
interjection, interval, intervene, introductive, fore-knowl-
edge, fore-seen, fore-shorten, fore-top, fore-lock, fore-
shadow, self-reproach, self-possession, self-denial, self-
conscious, self-confident, uncircumscribed, uninterested,
understand, undersigned, altogether.

QUESTIONS—LESSON No. 17.

1. What is represented by a light dot at the commencement of an outline? 2. What, by a heavy dot? 3. What does a light dash at the
beginning of a word represent? 4. What is said of *incon, uncom,* etc.,
when followed by *s?* 5. What distinction would you make between
recom and *irrecom?* 6. How would you write *in receipt?* 7. How is
noncom represented in noncompliance? 8. Write *misconstrued.* 9.
Contra, counter, etc., are represented by what? 10. What is said about
inter and *intro?* 11. What about *magne, magni,* etc? 12. How
would you write *foreseen?* 13. How may *self-con* be expressed? 14.
What is said about the joining of prefixes?

Lesson No. 18.

AFFIXES.

157. **Ing** may be denoted by a light dot at the end of the consonant outline, when the stroke is not more convenient ; thus,

tesing	saying	losing	showing	buying

1. **Ings** should be expressed by the stroke *Ing-Iss*, whenever it can be conveniently joined. In other cases a heavy dot may be used ; thus,

writings	sayings	meetings	holdings

2. **Ingly** may be denoted by a heavy tick at the end of the consonant outline ; thus,

amazingly	knowingly	charmingly	lovingly

3. **Ble, Bly,** when *Bel* can not be conveniently used, may be expressed by *b* joined.

4. **Bleness, Fullness, Someness** may be denoted by a small circle at the end of the consonant outline ; thus,

feebleness	faithfulness	lonesomeness	tangibleness

5. **Lessness** may be denoted by a large circle at the end of the consonant outline ; thus,

lawlessness   thanklessness   carelessness

6. **Ality, Ility, Erity,** etc. These terminations may be represented by disjoining the stroke immediately preceding them ; thus,

principality   disability   prosperity   stability

7. **For** and **Fore** terminating a word, may be represented by *f* joined : as *Ther-f,* for therefore ; *Wer-f,* for wherefore, etc.

8. **Ology** and **Alogy** may be represented by *j,* usually joined to the preceding part of the word ; thus,

phrenology   genealogy   zoology

9. **Ship** may be represented by *Ish* joined to, or written near the preceding part of the word ; thus,

partnership   hardship   penmanship

10. **Soever** may be denoted by *Iss-v* joined, or *Iss* disjoined ; thus,

wheresoever   whosoever   whithersoever   whosesoever

89

11. **Self** and **Selves** may be denoted, respectively, by a small and a large circle, joined if the junction is convenient ; thus,

myself	thyself	himself	ourselves

12 **Word-Signs** may frequently be used to advantage as *affix-signs ;* thus,

thereto	thereafter	wherever	whenever

READING EXERCISE.

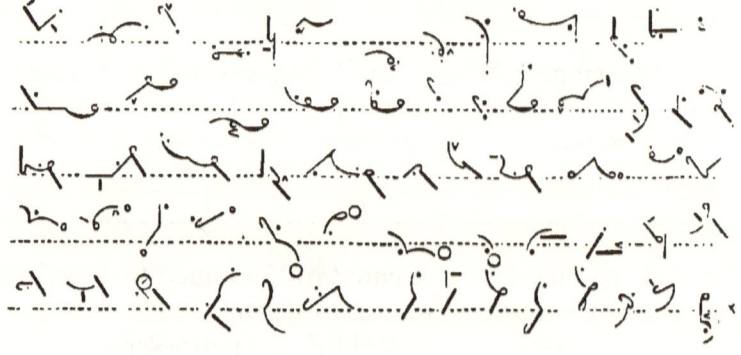

WRITING EXERCISE.

OMIT UNACCENTED VOWELS.

Boring, breaking, delaying, failing, baffling, defeating, alluring, talking, abusing, condensing, blessings, sufferings, fittings, paintings, savings, prancingly, seemingly, knowingly, laughingly, accountable, amendable, containable, diversible, fashionable, recognizable, lawfulness, knowableness, watchfulness, irksomeness, gladsomeness, slothfulness, groundlessness, artlessness, thoughtlessness, senselessness, boundlessness, frugality, popularity, sensibility, disability, instability, rascality, solvability, genealogy, geology, theological, mineralogy, courtship, consulship, seamanship, steamship, yourself, one's self, themselves.

QUESTIONS—LESSON No. 18.

1. What is generally used to represent the affix *ing*? 2. How many ways are there of representing *ings*? 3. When should the stroke be used? 4. How may *ble* and *bly* be expressed? 5. What is the difference between the signs for *fullness* and *lessness*? 6. How may *ality, erity*, etc., be expressed? 7. *For* and *fore* at the end of a word may be represented how? 8. *Ology* and *alogy*? 9. What is used to represent *ship* at the end of a word? 10. *Soever* may be expressed how? 11. *Self* and *selves*? 12. What is said about the use of word signs as affix-signs?

Lesson No. 19.

PHRASE-WRITING.

158. Joining two or more words without lifting the pen or pencil is called phrasing. Correct phrasing increases the speed of writing, and makes the notes more legible. Care must be taken to join only those words which naturally belong together; as,

| give me | this day | this side | do you |

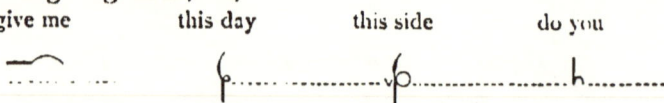

159. Observe the following rules:

1. Never join words that are not united in a phrase or clause.

2. Never join words unless the junction would be *clear*, *distinct*, and *easily formed*.

3. Do not employ *long* or *cumbersome* phrases.

POSITION OF PHRASES.

160. The first word usually determines the position of the phrase; that is, the first word is written in its proper place, and the others follow without regard to position; thus,

| it is not | we have seen | will be done | it is good |

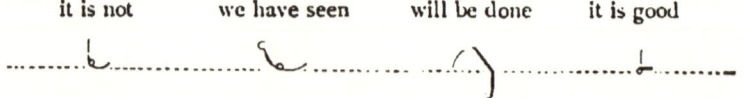

161　It is sometimes advantageous to raise or lower, slightly a first-place word, in order to bring the second word into its own position; thus,

in those	in these	by day	I had	I do

162.　When *as* begins a phrase it is sometimes better to adapt it to the position of the following word; thus,

as if	as to	as common	as if there were

163.　*A, an,* or *and,* beginning a phrase, takes the position of the word following, unless that word is *the, a, an,* or *and,* in which case it is written on the line; thus,

and in	and see	and but	and a	and the

OMISSION OF CONSONANTS.

164.　**P** may be omitted when immediately preceded by *m,* and followed by the *sound* of *t, k,* or *shon;* thus,

dumped	pumped	resumption	pumpkin

165.　**T** may be omitted when it follows *s* in such words as,

mostly	domestic	mistrustful	postoffice

93

166. **K** may be omitted when its sound occurs between *lng*, and *sh* or *shon;* frequently before final *shon*.

sanction   anxious   destruction   infraction

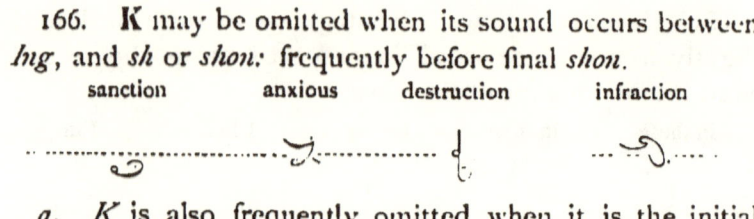

a. *K* is also frequently omitted when it is the initial consonant, and followed by *s;* hence we write *splen* for explain, *spet* for accept, *Iss-B-Shon* for exhibition, etc.

167. **N** may usually be omitted from the syllable *trans*, and from such words as *atonement, husbandman, passenger*, etc., where its representation would necessitate a difficult junction, or long outline, and where its omission would not endanger legibility.

atonement   husbandman   identical   passenger   messenger

168. **R** may be omitted from the syllable *scribe* in *prescribe, transcribe,* etc. Also in a few other cases, as in *manuscript, proportional*, etc.

a. It is allowable to omit any consonant whose expression would necessitate a difficult outline, and whose omission will not endanger legibility.

OMISSION OF WORDS.

169. **Of** or **of the,** between words, may be omitted and indicated by writing the word preceding and the word following *close to each other;* occasionally, by joining them; thus,

price of coal   days of the week   one of the greatest   bill of items

170. **To** or **To The** may be implied by writing the word following just under the line of writing,

| to-day | to know | to blacken | to say | to show |

The above is called the *fourth* position. *To* should not be implied before an up stroke, as *Ray*, *Lay*, *Hay*, etc., and is rarely implied before *k* or *g*.

171. **To,** preceding *have*, is sometimes omitted, where *have* can be expressed with a *V-hook;* thus,

| said to have | ought to have | was to have | they are to have |

172. **Have** may be omitted in phrase-signs when it precedes *been* and *done;* as,

| shall have been | shall have done | was to have been |

173. **A** or **and** may sometimes be safely and advantageously omitted from phrases; as,

| for a time | over and over | rich and poor | ever and ever |

174. **The** may be omitted when preceded by *to*, and followed by an up stroke; also in a few other cases; as,

| to the lake | to the races | to the house | in the world |

175. **From-to** may be omitted in such phrases as,

| from day to day | from season to season | from week to week |

176. **Or** may be omitted in such phrases as, *more or less, sooner or later;* or may also be implied between two numbers by writing one under the other; thus, $\frac{3}{4}$, *three or four*, etc.

177. In familiar work, the experienced phonographer will omit other words; but the student should confine himself, for some little time, to those here given. Experience will teach him how far he can safely go.

READING EXERCISE.

WRITING EXERCISE.

OMIT ALL VOWELS NOT NECESSARY TO CORRECT READING.

To the, on a, give a, it is, it is set, as soon as, (*Sez-us*) in time, for the weather, we are inclined, he will be glad, in the summer, it was, he will know, I remain, if there is any, I was there, you will do, there is nothing, in this way, there must be, there may be, would be certain, does not know, cannot do, he was there, I think he was, by those who, in hopes, and at a, in every respect, with those who, in this, in those, in this position, give it, give those, and should, of much greater, in this case, I had, as if there, as though, as to be, as usual, as few, as far, as she, and in the, and for the, and teach, a place, and a, and the.

Romped, co-emption, limped, attempt, stumped, Thompson, camped, lastly, vastly, mistake, justly, restless, postpone, conjunction, compunction, production, restriction, deflection, inflection, construction, attraction, affliction, translate, transmit, transcribe, transplant, manuscript, proportion.

Price of labor, fineness of the fabric, neatness of the writing, noise of the engine, one of the meanest, to-morrow, to advantage, to color, to compile, to instruct, five or six, eight or nine, big or little, large or small, dead or alive, I have been, we have been, may have done, will have been, never have been, black and white, summer and winter, red and white, to the road, to the shoulder, to the right, to the leader, to the rocks, from place to place, from city to city, from house to house, from street to street.

QUESTIONS—LESSON No. 19.

1. What is phrase-writing? 2. What is the object of phrasing? 3. Does phrasing impair legibility? 4. If a comma or pause of any kind occurs between two words, should they be joined? 5. What is said about joining, where the junction would be difficult or imperfect? 6. What word usually determines the position of the phrase? 7. What is the exception to this rule? 8. When may *p* be omitted? 9. When is it allowable to omit *t*? 10. When may *k* be omitted? 11. *N* is usually omitted from what syllable? 12. In what other cases may it be omitted? 13. When may *r* be omitted? 14. Are *of* and *of the* ever omitted? 15. When? 16. How may *to* or *to the* be implied? 17. What exception is there to this rule? 18. What is said about the omission of *or*? 19. Of *have*? 20. Of *a* or *and*? 21. What is said about the omission of *to* preceding *have*?

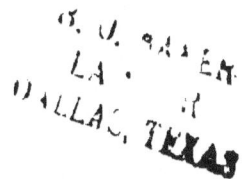

Lesson No. 20.

REPORTING EXPEDIENTS.

178. The speed of writing may be greatly increased by employing the following expedients. They should be so thoroughly memorized that they can be applied without the least hesitation.

179. **All** or **will** may be added by an *L* hook to any sign taking that hook; thus,

by all	they will	to all	and all	in all their

a. *All* or *will* may also be added to the simple *R* hook-signs by enlarging the hook; thus,

there will, they are all	which are all	from all

180. **Are** or **our** may be added by an *R* hook to any sign taking that hook; thus,

by our	which are	at our	but are

a. *Are* or *our* may also be added to the simple *L* hook-signs by enlarging the hook; thus,

for all are, or our	at all our	by all our

181. **Have** or **of** may be added by a V hook to signs taking that hook, also to the brief W word signs; thus,

| which have | all have | they have | were of | what have |

182. **Had, what** or **would** may sometimes be added to full length signs by halving them; thus,

it had, or would   in what, in it   had had   which had, or would

Perpendicular and inclined strokes, when so treated, are generally written in the third position.

183. **How** may be represented by a light tick just under the line, written upward or downward in the direction of *Ray* or *Chay;* thus,

how   how many   how much   how soon

184. **In** and **in the** may frequently be represented to advantage by an *In* hook; thus,

in the same place   in the construction   in the smallest

185. *In* may also be added to *here* and *there* by an N hook; as *Arn* for *here-in*, *Arn-Bef* for here-in-before.

186. **Ing thr** may be expressed by a heavy dash at the end of the preceding part of the word; thus,

facing their   eating their   raising their   placing their

a. No confusion will result between this and "*ingly*," as the context will indicate which is intended.

187. **Ing the, Ing a.** The affix *ing* and a following *the* may be expressed by a light dash, written at the end of the preceding stroke, in the direction of *p* or *Chay.* When *a,*

an, or *and* follows *ing*, the tick must be written perpendicularly or horizontally; thus,

paying the	showing the	paying a	showing an

188. **It** may frequently be added to a full length stroke by halving the stroke; thus,

if it	for it	until it	wish it

a. To the signs thus formed the small circle may be added to represent *is* or *has*.

189. **Is, as, has,** or **his** may be joined to a preceding or following word, beginning or ending with a circle, by enlarging the circle; thus,

as soon	has seen	as certain	pays his

190. **Not** may be added by an *N* hook to dash-vowel and half-length signs.

a. *Not* may also be added to full-length signs by halving them, and attaching the *N* hook; thus,

or not	ought not	if not	be not	have not

191. **Numbers.** The following method will greatly facilitate the rapid expression of figures.

20	30	40	50	60	70	80	90

a. In expressing round numbers, write *Ned* for hundred, *Ith*[3] for thousand, and *Mel*[1] for million; thus,

300	6,000	7,000,000	300,000	40,000

b. In writing dollars and cents, omit both dollar sign and decimal point; thus,

four hundred sixty-seven dollars, twenty-nine cents.

467 ^{29}

c. Solid figures, as three thousand four hundred seventy-seven, are expressed best in the ordinary way; thus,

3477

192. **Own** may be added by an *N* hook to a *full-length,* or *lengthened curve* stroke.

a. *Own* may also be added by an *N* hook to any stroke to which *our* or *their* has been added; thus,

our own   my own   in their own   at our own   by their own

193. **One** may often be advantageously added by an *N* hook; thus,

any one   at one   another one   each one

a. In practice, no confusion will result from representing *own* and *one* by the same hook, as the context will clearly indicate the word.

194. **Past Tense.** Many phonographers frequently write the present tense for the past, depending upon the context to denote which was intended; as, *demand* for *demanded*, *regard* for *regarded*, etc.

a. The extent to which this principle may be carried with safety will depend upon the aptness of the writer; all can safely use it in familiar matter.

195. **Syllables disjoined.** It is sometimes con-

102

venient to disjoin two parts of a word, writing them close together; thus,

draughtsman   non-forfeitable   non-payment

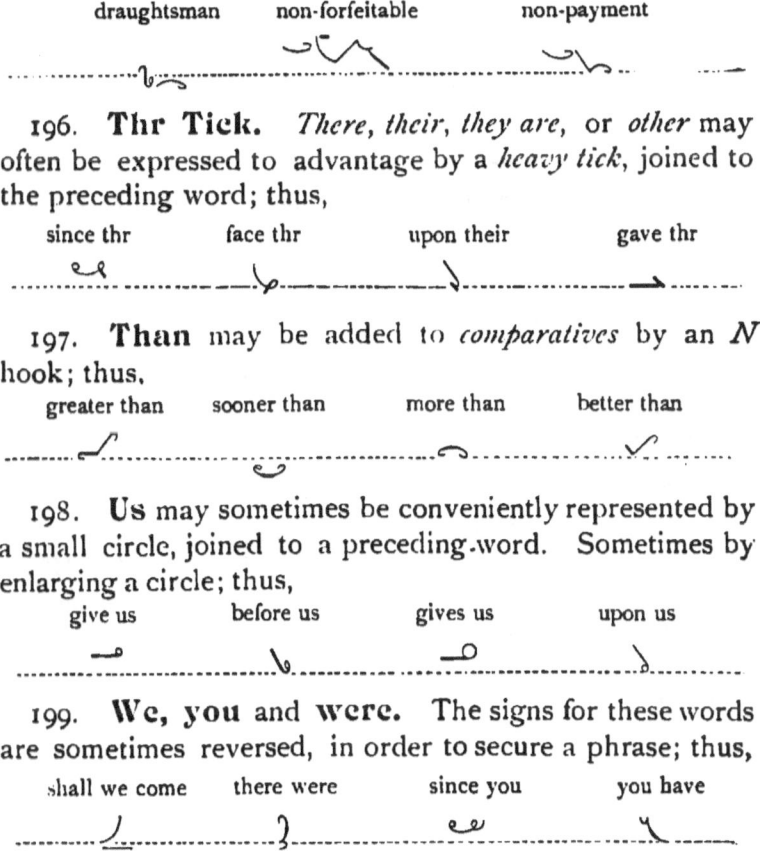

196. **Thr Tick.** *There, their, they are,* or *other* may often be expressed to advantage by a *heavy tick*, joined to the preceding word; thus,

since thr   face thr   upon their   gave thr

197. **Than** may be added to *comparatives* by an *N* hook; thus,

greater than   sooner than   more than   better than

198. **Us** may sometimes be conveniently represented by a small circle, joined to a preceding word. Sometimes by enlarging a circle; thus,

give us   before us   gives us   upon us

199. **We, you** and **were.** The signs for these words are sometimes reversed, in order to secure a phrase; thus,

shall we come   there were   since you   you have

BRIEF W AND Y ENLARGED.

A brief *W* or *Y* word-sign, followed by another brief *W* or *Y* word-sign, is of frequent occurrence. Mr. Graham, in

his Hand-Book, treats of these in the following very appro;
priate manner.

1. Enlarging a brief *W* sign adds a brief *W* word-sign;
thus,

we were or we would	were we or were what	what would, what we, or what were
⊂	⊂	⊃

2. Writing an enlarged brief *W* sign, in the direction of
Ray, denotes an added brief *Y* word-sign; thus,

with you	were you	would you
ᴜ	ᴜ	∩

3. Enlarging a brief *Y* denotes an added brief *W* or *Y*
word-sign; thus,

ye were	you would	you were	beyond you
∪	∩	∪	∩

4. **Names.** *Weh* and *Wuh*, enlarged in their natural
direction, are called, respectively, *Weh-Weh* and *Wuh-Wuh*.
When written in the direction of *Ray*, they may be called
Weh-Yuh and *Wuh-Yuh*.

Yeh and *Yuh* enlarged may be called *Yeh-Weh* and
Yuh-Wuh.

To the Student.

You have now been over all the principles, and it is presumed that you have a good knowledge of them. Much work, however, remains to be done before you will acquire sufficient speed to do practical work. Let your motto be *practice, practice, practice.* Remember, too, that speed does not come from mere writing, but from intelligent study combined with it.

In your writing thus far you have expressed all, or nearly all the vowel sounds. You should now omit them entirely, except where the insertion of one is necessary to the correct reading of the word. Great care should be taken, however, to write the outline in the position denoted by the accented vowel.

Apply all the "Reporting Expedients." Do not use a long outline where a short one will do as well. Do not write "of," "of the," "to," or "to the," where you can imply them. These are little things in themselves, but they make a great difference in one's speed.

The following pages are given as samples for your guidance. It would be well to study the first one till you can read it readily; then write it over and over, each time trying to write a little faster than you did the preceding time, yet never faster than you can form the characters well. After you have practiced the first one faithfully, take the second, and after this, the third.

A portion of each day should be given to memorizing the "Brief Word-Forms," beginning on page 113. Practice these till you can write them at a high rate of speed.

Jas. H. Cole

4-17-91

29 Nunda

451 Main St., Buffalo, N. Y.,
Apr. 17, 1891.

Mr. Jas. H. Cole,
Box 29, Nunda, N. Y.

My dear Sir:

I am in receipt of your letter of the 13th inst., and am pleased to learn that your progress has been so rapid. Let me caution you, however, to be very sure that you understand the principles thoroughly. If you do, and can apply them readily, you may congratulate yourself on having accomplished the first, and perhaps most important step in the study of Short-hand; if you do not, review carefully from the very beginning of the book. Any attempt at further progress before the principles have been mastered will be quite likely to result in failure.

Resolve to become a good stenographer. The market is overstocked with poor ones. It will pay you to put forth earnest and persistent effort, as the higher speed you obtain, and the more proficient you make yourself, the better place and the larger salary you will be able to secure. Make it a practice, not only to read over a large portion of everything you write, but to make frequent transcripts, exercising the utmost care in spelling, punctuating and capitalizing. These are very important, and if you find yourself deficient in this part of the work, take immediate steps to remedy the defect. The demand for competent stenographers was never so great as at the present time, and you need have no fear that your services will not be needed, if you prove yourself capable. Do not, however, expect a position until you can do good, and fairly rapid work.

Yours truly,

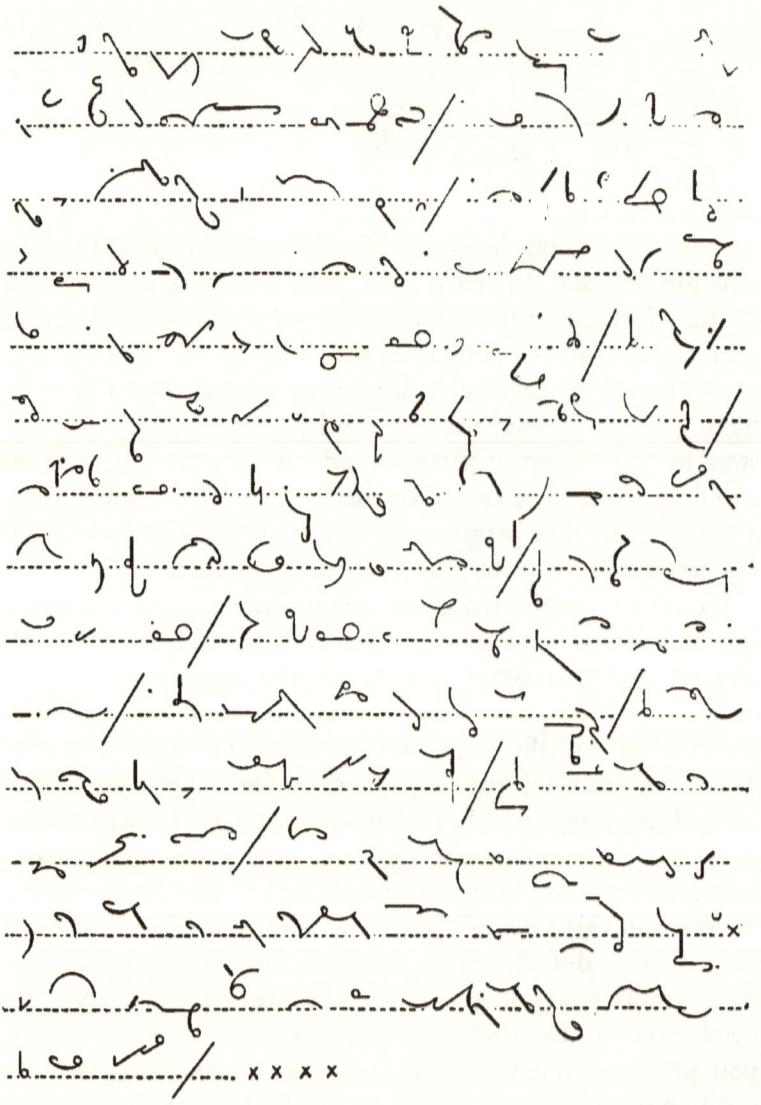

CHAUNCEY M. DEPEW,

To the Yale Law Students.

I do not propose to pursue any of the subjects upon which you have been instructed by this learned faculty, nor am I prepared to compete with you with a thesis upon some legal question, as a part of the exercises of graduation. The commencement orator usually addresses himself to the professors and the elder members of the profession, but I am here to speak to you. The most joyous of days is that which closes the doors of the school, and opens the gate-way to the world; the most apprehensive, the one which marks the opening of your clientless office; the happiest, the first return, after the future is secure and success assured, to college scenes and associations. It is the privilege of age and experience to indicate paths in the field you are yet to explore, to point out the dangers which beset them, and the methods of safe and comfortable travel. Most of the ideals of these closing hours, devoted to the confidential interchange of aspirations and hopes, will be shattered against the stern realities of practical life, but their destruction will furnish the lessons for sure foundations and permanent construction.

At this hour, all your thoughts are concentrated in one word, *success*. If your construction of success were honestly analyzed, it would probably mean, to most minds, the getting of money. The desire to acquire property is the most potent force in the activities of our people. It is the mainspring of our marvelous development, and the incentive and reward of intelligent industry. · It is alike the cause of the noblest efforts and the most revolting crimes. That man would be unfaithful to his family, and to his own independence, who did not use every honorable effort, and practice every reasonable economy, to secure home and competence for declining years. But the lawyer who makes this his sole aim is an unworthy member of the noblest of professions, and will never win its honors or rewards. * * * *

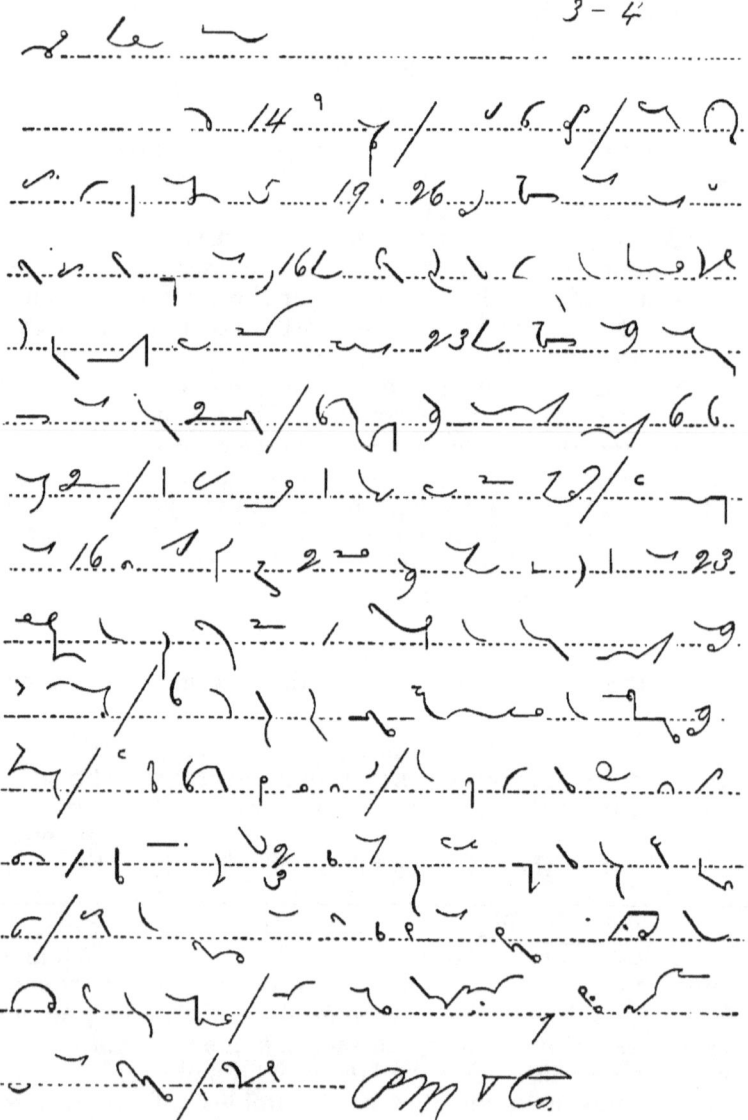

The Saturday Globe,

A CHOICE FAMILY WEEKLY.

Circulation 152,000.

P. MARTIN & CO., PROPS.

St. Louis, March 4th, 1891.

Messrs. Johnson & King,
   West 14th St., New York City.

Gentlemen:
            Yours is just at hand. In reply will say that we
ran your "Ad." in the December 5th, 19th, and 26th issues,
and then again in the New Year number; but were not able
to get it in the issue of the 16th of January, as that number was full before your order for continuance was received;
so it had to be carried one week later, and went in the
23rd of January, and then again in the first issue in February, and again in the February 20th number. This will
be followed by the first issue in March, March 6th, then
in the issue of the 20th. It really carries it forward one
week on each insertion. We could not get it in the 16th,
as you originally wished it, and which would have been
two weeks after the first issue in January, but could use
it in the 23rd, and since that time have used it every other
week, which brings it, for February and March, in the
first issues of the month. These are both especially good
numbers, and we have many calls for extra copies of the
first issues of each month. We trust this will be satis-
factory and as you wished it.
            If, during your best season, you would run some
large "Ads." giving us the option of two or three dates in
which to use them when we could do the best for them, we
believe it would pay you well. We are not able, ever, to
promise any particular dates, except in the special numbers; the regular issues being always full far in advance.
Kindly notify us by return mail how much space you are
likely to need in the April numbers.
                  Very respectfully,

                     P. Martin & Co.

BRIEF WORD-FORMS.

The following list of Brief Word-forms should be thoroughly memorized. The student who has mastered the principles as he has gone along will have comparatively little difficulty in committing these forms to memory. They should be gone over again and again, until they can be written at the rate of at least one hundred a minute, and read quite as rapidly. Perfect familiarity with them will enable one to write much faster, and with considerably less effort, than would otherwise be required.

The words have been very carefully selected, and are such as will occur in almost any kind of amanuensis or reporting work. The outlines of many of the words, if written in full, would be exceedingly cumbersome and inconvenient ; in other cases confliction would result, and the accuracy of the notes would be impaired.

BRIEF WORD-FORMS.

A

able to have		annual
absurd-ity		another-one
accept-ed-ation		any one
acceptable		any other one
acquaintance		annihilate
accident		anybody
addition		anticipate-d-ion
adjournment		appear
adjustment		appearance
administrator		apply
admit-ted-tance		appliance
advancement		application
adventure		applicant
advertise-ed-ment		apprehend-ed
agent		(in phrasing) are
all of, all have		arrive al
long, along		artificial
amount-ed		as it ought
and all, and will		as great as
and of, and have		as long
angel		as little

. . . . . as the	....⌣.... . . avoid-ed-ance, of it
. . . as it, has it	....ι.... . . . . . . awful-ness
. . assemble-d-y	**B**
. . . assignment	.⟍⌢. . . . . barometer-rical
. . assist-ed-ance	.⟍.. . . . . . . bank-able
. . . . assistant	⟍ . . . . bankrupt-cy
. . . . associate	...⟍... . . . . beauty-ful
. . . . . at first	...⟍... . . . . before it
. . . at hand	...⌐.... . . . . . begin-ning
. . . . at length	..⌐... . . . . begun
. . . . . . at our	.... began
. at our own	..⌐.. . . . . behind
. . . at it, it had	..ʮ.. . . . . . . behindhand
. . . . . attain	..S.. . . . . . . behold
. . . attainment	⟍.. . . . . belief
at the same time	⟍.. . . . . belong
. . at sometime	..⟍.. . . . . . . believe
. authority-ative	.⟍.. . . . . . beneficence-nt
. . . . . averse	...⟍.. . . . . be not
. . . . aversion	.⟍.. . . . . betake
. . . . average	...ʃ.... . . . . . . bold-ness

. . . complete	...?... . . . . . constitute-ed
. . . completion	...ℓ... . . . . constitution-al
. . . compliance	...ᑫ... . . . . . .construct-ed
. . . comply-ied	...ᑫ... . . . . . . construction
. comprehend-ed	...ᑕ... in (or in the) construction
comprehension-ive	...⌒... . . . . . . .consume
. . . . concern	...⌒... . . . . . consumption
. . . .conclude	...J... . . . . contain
. . . concluded	...⌐... . . . . . contract-ed
. . . conclusion	...ᑐ... . . . . . . contraction
. conclusive-ness	...L... . . . .contradict-ed-ory
. . condition-al	...ᑐ... . . . . . contradiction
. . . . congress	...ᑐ... . . . . . contrive-ance
. conscientious-ly	...⌐... . . . . . . control-led
. . consequence	...ᒐ... . . . . . .controversy
. . . consequent	...ᒐ... . . . . . converse-ant
consider-able-ness	...ᒐ... . . . . . . convert-ed
. considerate-ness	...⌐... . . . correct-ed-ness
. . . . . consist	...⌐... . . . . . . correction
. . . consistence	...⌐... . . . . corrects
. . . constituent	...ᒪ... counsel for the defense

117

...⌐... counsel for the defendant

...⌐... , counsel for the plaintiff

... . countenance-ed

— . . . . country

... . countryman

... . countrymen

... . county

... . court

... . . cross-examine-ation

... . cure

... . cures-curious

D

...? . . . . danger

...? . . . . dangers-ous

...? . . . . dark

...? . . . . darken-ed

...? . . . . Dear Sir

...? . . . . . Dear Madam

...? . . . . . December

...? . . . . defeat

...? . . . . defendant

...? . . . . defense-ive

...? . . . . defer

...? . . . . . deficient-cy

...? . . . . deform-ed-ity

...? . . . . . defraud-ed

...? . . . . . degeneration

...? . . . . degree

...? . . . . . delight-ed

...? . . . . delinquent-cy

...? . . . . delinquents

...? . . . . deliver-ed-y

...? . . . . . deliverance

...? . . democrat-ic-cy

...? . . denominate-d-ion

...? . . . . . depravity

...? . . derived-derivative

...? . . . derive-derivation

...? . . . . . . determine

...? . . . determination

...? . . . . develop-ment

...? . . . . . . describe d

. . . . description	. . . . during it
. . . . . direct-ed	**E**
. . . . . direction	. . . . each will
. . . . directness	. . . . each one
. . . . . discharge	. . . . efficient
dissatisfy ied-action	. . . . enlarged
dyspeptic-sia	. . . . . . England
. . . distinct	. . English
. distinctive	. . . . . enthusiasm
distinguish-ed	. . . . . . essential
District of Columbia	. . . . . . evening
. . divine	. . . . . every one
. . . . . . doctor	. . . . . evident-ce
. . . . . doctrine	. . . . exact-ed-ness
. . . . dollar	. . . exaggerate-d
. . . . . down thr	. . exaggeration
. . . . . downfall	. . . . examine
. . . downcast	. . . . example
. . . . dread ed	. . . . . . except-ed
. . . . . drunken	. . . . . . exception
. . . drunkenness	. . . . . executor

. . . . exchange-d	. . . . fail
. . . . exclusive-ness	. . . . failure
. . . . exhibit	. . . . fall
. . . . exhibition	. . . . . fallen, fall in
. . . . expect-ed-ation	. . . . false
. . . . . expend-iture	. . . . family
. . . . expended	. . . . fault-y
. . . . expense-ive-ness	. . . . favor-ed
. . . . . . experience	. . . . February
in (or in the) experience	. . . . . feature, if it
. . . explain-atory-ation	. . . . feel
. . . . explained	. . . . feel it
. . . . . explicit-ness	. . . . felt
. . . . explore-d-ation	. . . . fell in
. . . . . express-ed-ive	. . . . financial
. . . . exquisite	. . . . footstep
. . . . . extraordinary	. . . . . . for instance
. . . . extravagant-ce	. . : . . . . for all
. . . . extreme	. . . . . . for all are
F	. . . . for the plaintiff
. . . . fact	. . for the defendant

120

_____ . for all it, or for all had

.... form-ed

.... formal·ity

.... formation

.... former-ly

.... formless

.... found·ed·ation

.... fortune·ate·ly

.... fraction

.... freedom

.... frequency

.... frequent

.... from all

.... fuller

.... frank-ness

.... Franklin

.... frantic

.... from one

.... from it

.... furnish-ed-ture

.... future-ity

G

.... give it

.... gave it

.... glory, glorify

.... glorious

.... govern·ment

.... governor

.... grandchild

.... granddaughter

.... grandson

.... Great Britain

.... guilt-y

H

.... habeas corpus

.... had had, or it

.... happy

.... happiness

.... has known

.... have·ing been

.... henceforth

.... heretofore

....	history·ical
....	holy
....	holier
....	holiest
....	horticulture·al
....	House of Representatives
....	hopeful·ness

I

....	I am in receipt of your letter
....	idle·ness
....	if all are, or our
....	identical
....	if the court please
....	ignorance
....	ignorant
....	illegible·ity
....	imagine·ary·ation
....	imaginative
....	imagined
....	immoral·ity
....	immortal·ity
....	immortalize
....	impatience
....	impatient
....	improper·ly·riety
....	in all
....	indefatigable
....	indenture
....	independent
....	indescribable
....	indignant
....	individual
....	inhabit·ed·ant
....	inquire
....	insignificant
....	instant
....	integrity
....	intellectual
....	in (or in the)consideration
....	inconsiderate·ness
....	information
....	informed·inform·ant

122

. . . . in it	) . . . . is there
. . in one, any one	) . . . . is it
. . . . in our	. .) . . . . issue
. . . . in relation	.) . . . . issued
. in reply to your letter	. . ⌠ . . . . is just at hand
. in reply to your favor	. . .	. . . . . it had or would
. . . . . . inscribe-d	. . .	. . . it had or would not
. . . . . inscription	.	. . . . it ought
. . . . . . insecure	J . . . . . . it ought not
. . . . . in so far as	L . . . . . it ought to have
. . . in the first place	L . . it ought to have had
(or in the) second place	. .	. . . . it would have had
. . . . interior	. .	. . . . itself

J

. . interpret-ed-ation	
. . . . . . intestate	∠ . . . . January
. . . . . intolerable	ℓ . . . . Jehovah
. . . . . invite-ation	/ . . . . Jesus
. . . . . irreligious	∠ . . . Jesus Christ
. . is known, or none	∠ . . . . Jesus of Nazareth
. . . . is said	∠ . . . . . . joint stock
. . . is said to have	/ . . . . judicial

123

. . . . judiciary

. . . judicious-ly-ness

. . . . jury

. . . . . . jurisdiction

. . . . just as

. . . . justice

. . . . . . justify-iable

. . . . . just at hand

. . . . . just received

L

. . ladies and gentlemen

. . . . large

. . . . larger

. . . . largest

. . . . . . learn-ed

. . . . . learned counsel

. . . . . learned judge

. . . . . legislate-d-ation

. . . . . . legible-ity

. . . . . . illegible-ity

. . . . length

. . . . lengthy

. . . . lengthen

. . . . . . lengthened

. . . . little

. . . . long

. . . . . . longer

M

. . . . machine

. . . . . . machinist

. . . . . . machinery

. . . . may have been

may it please your honor

. may it please the court

. . . . magnet-ic-ism

. . . . . . majority

. . . manufacture-r-ory

. . . . Massachusetts

. . . . mechanic-al-ism

. . . . Mediterranean

. . . memoranda-um

. . . . . mental-ity

124

. mention

. mentioned

. mercy-iful

merchandise

. messenger

. metropolitan

. metropolis

. microscope-ic-al

. might-y

. million-th

. misfortune

. mistake

. moral-ity

. movement

. mortal-ity

. mortgage

. mortgagee

. My dear Sir

N

. next

. next time

. next day

. neglect

New Jersey

. . New York

. New York City

. New York State

. . . nobody

North Carolina

. . November

. . no one

. no other

. no other one

O

. obligation

. obligatory

. occur

. occurred

. occurrence

. of it

. of thr

. often-times

....⌐.... . . . . . . ofttimes	—⌐. . . party of the first part
.....⌐... . . . omnipotent·ce	..⌐.... party of the second part
....)....... . . . . on either hand	..⌐... . . . . partake
...)... . . . on the other hand	....⌐ . . . . passenger
...⌐... on (or on the) one hand	....⌐.... . . . . . . people
...⌐.... . .one other, or another	⌐... . . . . perfect
...⌐... . . . . only	⌐... . . . . . perfected
...⌐.... . . . . . opposition	⌐... . . . . . perfection
...⌐.... . . . . oppression	....⌐.... . . . . . Pennsylvania
....⌐.... . . . . . . order	...⌐... . . . perform·ed·ance
...⌐.... . . . . . . ordinary	....⌐.... . . permanent·ly·ce
....⌐.... . . . . . . organ	⌐... . . . perpendicular·ity
....⌐.... . . . . . organize	...⌐... . . . . person
....⌐.... . . . . organization	...⌐... . . philanthropy·ic·ist '
....⌐.... . . . . . over it	...⌐.... . . . phenomena·on·al
....⌐.... . . . . . . overtake	...⌐... . . . . . Philadelphia
P	....⌐.... . . photography·ic·er
...⌐.... . . . . . preliminary	....⌐.... . . . . . . popular·ity
...⌐.... . . . . parallel	...⌐.... . . . . . . power
...⌐... . . . . parliament·ary	...⌐... . ,. . . . powerful
...⌐... . . . party, patent·ed	...⌐.... . . . . practice

......`\o`..... . . . . present	.....`/\`.... . . . . reform-ed-atory
...`\`... . . . . . . prejudice-d	....`/`.... . . . . religion
...`\`... . . prepare-d-atory-ation	....`/`.... . . . . religious
....`\`.... . . . . . . Presbyterian	....`\~`.... . . . relinquish-ed-ment
...`\`.... . . . . pretty	....`\~`.... . . . . . remonstrate-d
.....`\`.... . . . . . . prima-facie	...`/\`.... . . . . . . republican
...`\`.... . . . . professor	...`/\`.... . . . . . repute-d-ation
.....`\`.... . . . . profit-ed	...`/\`.... . . . respect-ed-ing-ful
...`\`.... . . . . . . proof-prove	....`\`.... . . . . retake
.....`\`.... . . . . . prominent-ce	...`/\`.... . . . . . . revenge-d
....`\`.... . . . . property	...`/`.... . . . . . . reveal-ed
...`\`.... . . . . . . proportion	...`/`.... . . . . . . revelation
...`\`.... . . . . . . protection	....`/`.... . . . . . revolution
....`\`.... . . . . . . production	....`/`.... . . . . . rhetoric-al
....`\`.... . . . . punish-ed-ment	...`/`.... . . . . rule-d
....`\`.... . . . . purpose	...`\`.. . . . . Roman Catholic
R	**S**
`/`..... . . . . real-ity	...`(`.... . . . . . said to have
`/`..... . . . . realize	...`/`... . . . . . . salvation
`/`..... . . . recollect-ed-ion	...`o_`... . . . . . San Francisco
`/`..... . . . . . . recover-ed	....`/`.... . . . . . . satisfy-ied

127

. . . . . satisfaction	. . . . . . so far as
. . . . . . scripture-al	. . . . . . sometime
. . . Secretary of State	. . . . . . south-east
. . . Secretary of War	. . . . south-eastern
. . . . scientific	. . . . . . southern
. . . . . scoundrel-ism	. . . . south-western
. . . . . . September	. . . . . south-west
. . . . serious	. . . . . south-wester
. . . . set off	. . speak, superior-ity
. . . . set forth	. . . . . . speaker
. . . . shall it	. . . . . . special-ty
. . she had, she would	. . . . . spiritual-ity
. . . . . . signify-ied	. . . spiritualism
. . . significant-ce-cy	. . . spiritualistic
. . . . . signification	. . . . . spontaneous
. . . . . . similar-ity	. . . . . . standard
. . . . . simple-icity	. . . . . . statistic
. . . . . . single-d	. . . stepping-stone
. . . . . singular-ity	stenography-er-ic
. . . . . . situation	. . . . . . stranger
. . . . . . skillful	. . . . . . strength

. . . stupendous-ness

. . . . . . stupid-ity

. . . . . sublime-ity

. subordinate-d-ation

. . . . . substantial

. substantiate-d-ation

. . . . substitute-d

. . . . . . such had

such had, or would not

. such ought to have

such ought to have had

. . such would have

. . . sufficient-cy-ly

. . . suggest-ed-ion

. . superintend-ed-ent

. . . . superior-ity

. . . . supreme-acy

. . . . . swindle-d-r

. . . . take

. . . . take it

. . . . taken

. . . . tendency

. . . . . . telegraph·ic

. . . . . . testament-ary

. . . . testify

. . . . , that thr

. . . . . thanksgiving

. . . . . . thenceforth

. . . . . there ought

there ought to have been

. . . . the other

. . . . . . there will

. . there would or had

. . . . . they are all

. . . they had or would

. . . . . they had not

. . . . . thousand-th

. . . . . to have been

. . . . tolerate-d-ation

. . . . . tolerance

. . . . took

. . . . . . transient

129

Shorthand	Word
	twelve-fth
	tragedy
	trans-Atlantic
	transcend-ed
	transfer-red
	transform-ed

U

Shorthand	Word
	under
	United States
	universe-al
	universalism
	university
	unless
	uniform
	unimagined

V

Shorthand	Word
	vegetate-d-ion
	vegetable-rian
	vengeance
	vice-versa
	Virginia

Shorthand	Word
	virtue
	virtuous
	virtuously
	visible

W

Shorthand	Word
	warrant-ed-able
	was to have
	was thr
	we are in receipt of your valued favor
	we are to have
	we know
	we have known
	welcome
	we made
	we may be
	we may have been
	we may, with me or my
	we may not, we meant
	we mention
	were it

.... were made

.... were meant

.... were mentioned

.... were no

.... what is your occupation

.... where do you reside

.... where it

.... which are to have

.... which had or would not

.... which ought to have

which ought to
have had, or it

.... which ought not

.... which have had

.... which will it

.... which will not

.... which would have

which would
have had or it

.... while it

.... wish it

.... with him

.... women

.... woman

.... work-ed

.... workman-men

Y

.... year-s

.... yes sir

.... your valued favor

.... your letter at hand

.... your communication

.... your esteemed favor

Practice Letters for Students.

LETTER OF APPLICATION.

341 Watson St.,
May 3, 1891.

The James Jackson Co.,
        City.

Gentlemen :

        Mr. Hany informs me that you are desirous of securing the services of an amanuensis. I have recently completed a thorough course in short-hand under the direction of Prof. Chase, and wish to procure employment.

    I am permitted to refer you to the above named gentlemen; also to Mr. Cassel, President of the Marine Bank.

    Hoping for a favorable response, I am,

            Respectfully,

                    HENRY KEEFER.

LETTER OF APPLICATION.

39 Maryland Ave.,

March 29, 1891.

Messrs. Harris & Bro.,

14 Board of Trade Bldg., City.

Gentlemen:

I am desirous of securing a position as stenographer, and am informed that there is a vacancy in your office.

Should you desire an interview, I shall be pleased to call at such time as you may designate.

References.

Barnes, Hengerer & Co.,

John T. Noye Mfg. Co.,

Tonawanda Lumber Co., Tonawanda, N. Y.

Respectfully,

MAUD EMERSON.

COMMENDATORY LETTER, (Special).

Office of

H. B. CLAFLIN & CO.,

New York, April 20, 1891.

Messrs. Wood & Co.,

Chicago, Ills.

Gentlemen:

Your letter of the 18th is before us. We can recommend Mr. Harvey Hale as a young man of unusual ability, and strict business integrity. He has been in our employ, as stenographer, for three years, during the past two of which he has had entire charge of the correspondence, and has filled this difficult position with perfect satisfaction.

Yours truly,

H. B. CLAFLIN & CO.

COMMENDATORY LETTER, (General.)

COLLEGE OF BUSINESS,

Coleman, N. Y., April 27, '91.

To the Business Public :

      This is to certify that Miss Jennie Hood is a graduate of the Short-hand Department of this Institution. She has a speed of about one hundred thirty-five words per minute on miscellaneous matter, and can transcribe her notes rapidly and accurately. During the time spent under our direction we have always found her punctual, and ready to perform any task imposed upon her.

      Respectfully,

LETTER OF INTRODUCTION, (Business.)

.

JAMES' BUSINESS COLLEGE,

Bennett, N. Y., May, 1891.

John Mooney, Esq.,

Johnstown, Pa.

Dear Sir :

This will introduce to you Mr. David E. Bell, the young man we send in answer to your application for a stenographer. Mr. Bell is well prepared, and we are sure you will find him, in every way, a desirable assistant.

Yours truly,

JAMES BROS.

LETTER OF INTRODUCTION, (Social.)

Grand Rapids, Mich.,

April 23, 1891.

Dear Charles,

This will introduce to you my much esteemed friend, Mr. George Reed.   He is taking a business trip to New York, and I have persuaded him to spend a day with you.   I have pictured in glowing terms your beautiful home and genial hospitality, and I bespeak for him a very enjoyable time.

Yours very truly,

J. C. WINTER.

Dr. Charles Meade,
Cleveland, Ohio.

LETTER ORDERING GOODS.

Summit, Pa.,
Apr. 13, 1891.

Messrs. Granger & Co.,
Philadelphia, Pa.

Gentlemen :

Please ship at once, by fast freight, the following :

15 boxes M. Soap.
5 chests Best Oolong Tea.
10 bbls. Granulated Sugar.
3 " Light Brown Sugar.

We wish you would exercise special care in the selection of the tea, as our customers complained that the last lot was not up to the usual standard.

Draw at 30 days' sight for amount of bill.

Respectfully,

J. O. WAKEFIELD.

Guide to the Use of Capitals.

The following rules for the use of capitals have been very carefully prepared, and, with the copious illustrations, will be found of much assistance to the young stenographer.

1. **Every Sentence and Every Line of Poetry** should begin with a capital.

2. **Proper Names** should begin with capitals; as, *John* and *James* went to the *White Mountains.* The city of *Cincinnati* is on the *Ohio* river.

3. **Proper Adjectives** and **Words derived from Proper Names** should begin with capitals; as, *American, Roman, Bostonian, Swedish, Smithsonian, to Christianize.*

4. **Direct Quotations.**—When the exact words of a speaker or writer are used, the first word should begin with a capital; as, James said, *"Come with me."*

5. The pronoun *I* and the interjection *O* should be capitals.

6. **Names of God,** words denoting or referring to the Deity should begin with capitals; as, "Trust in *Providence.*" "For in *Thee, O Lord* do I hope." "*Thou* wilt hear, *O Lord* my *God.*" "Trust in *Him* and *He* will give you rest." *Jehovah, Creator, Almighty.*

7. **Months of the Year, Days of the Week, Holidays, and Special Seasons** should begin with capitals; as, *January*, *Monday*, *Christmas*, *Fourth of July*, *Good Friday*, *Lent*, *Advent*, *Trinity*.

Spring, summer, fall, autumn, and *winter*, should not be capitalized unless personified.

8. **Titles of Honor and Office** should begin with capitals; as, *Dr.; Mr.; Rev.; General Hood; Sergeant Mills; Peter Chase, D. D., LL. D.; Hon James Drew; President Madison; His Honor, the Mayor.*

9. **Names Personified.** The name of anything spoken of as a person should begin with a capital; as, "Come gentle *Spring*," "Then *Hope* said."

10. **In Headings and Titles** the important words, (usually nouns, pronouns, adjectives, verbs, and adverbs) should be capitalized; as, *"An Illustrated History of the State of Vermont,"* Pope's *"Essay on Man,"* "His *Majesty, Myself.*"

In books, the titles and heads of the principal divisions are printed in small capitals.

11. **Names Composed of Proper and Common Nouns;** such as, *Junior course, Cayuga creek, Andes mountains,* etc., should have the first word only capitalized, (unless used in a title or in an address) because it may be used alone. In such names as *Rocky Mountains, Jersey City, Black Hills,* etc., both parts should be capitalized, as both are necessary to describe the place.

12. **Religious Sects, Political Parties, Organizations, Societies and Companies** should begin with capitals; as *Methodist, Catholic, Republican, Prohibition*

party, Band of Hope, Radicals, Conservatives, The Courier Co.

13. **Distinct Regions ;** as, *Pacific Coast, the North, the Southwest, North Siberia, etc.,* should be capitalized. In the sentence, *He was traveling west,* west should not be capitalized as it denotes simply direction.

In the sentence, *He went West,* west should begin with a capital, as it here denotes a certain part of the country.

14. **Words of Special Importance** describing great events, or special things which have acquired a distinct name should be capitalized ; as, *Blue Monday, Gulf Stream, the Dark Ages, the Revolution, the Civil War.*

15. It is sometimes allowable to capitalize a word in order to give it special emphasis ; as, Write every *Proper Name,* and every *Adjective* derived from a *Proper Noun* with an initial-capital.—*Swinton's Grammar.*

16. In display advertisements, important words are generally capitalized. It is also customary in writing amounts in checks, notes, etc., to capitalize each word ; as, *Four Hundred Thirty ;* also different items and important words in bills ; as, 3 lbs. *Tea,* 4 bu. *Potatoes,* etc.

Punctuation.

Punctuation is so important a part of the education of the stenographer, and so few have a practical knowledge of the art, that it has been thought advisable to give in this book a series of rules which, it is hoped, will be found of great benefit to the stenographer, and enable him to render better transcripts than he otherwise could.

THE COMMA.

The comma denotes the least of the divisions of a sentence. The following rules will show its principal uses.

RULE 1. When words or phrases are not essential to the meaning or structure of the sentence in which they stand, but are merely thrown in, as it were, they should usually be set off by commas ; as, It is said, *however*, that the conditions are favorable. He has just heard, *evidently*, of the late disaster. A practical education is, *in fact*, the key to success. He went, *accordingly*, and made arrangements.

RULE 2. **Clauses** or **Phrases** coming between the subject and predicate of a sentence, or between any of its principal parts, should usually be set off by commas.

The painter has, *with perfect reality*, depicted the horrors of war.

"The sun, *with all its train of attendant planets*, is but a small portion of the universe.

John, *who had studied faithfully*, secured the prize.

The book, *though not a new one*, was highly prized.

RULE 3. **The Ellipsis of a Verb** should be marked by a comma ; as, James went to France; John, to England. He has one book ; she, two. Commas indicate the closest connection ; brackets, the remotest.

RULE 4. **Relative Clauses, not Restrictive,** should usually be set off by commas.

EXAMPLES.

The young man, *who seemed very bright*, found ready employment.

They intend to go in the spring, *which is the most delightful season of the year in that country.*

The giant trees of California, *which are the largest in the world*, are falling victims to man's greed.

NOTE 1. A clause is restrictive when it limits the meaning of some particular word to some particular sense ; as, Books *which are full of knowledge* are valuable. Here the author does not say that all books are valuable, but merely those that are full of knowledge. The clause is, therefore, restrictive, and should not be set off by commas. Some authors would, however, place a comma after knowledge to mark the logical subject.

NOTE 2. If several words come between the relative and its antecedent, a comma should precede the relative even if it is used restrictively ; as, He is the best man, who does the most good.

NOTE. 3. A comma should always be placed before the relative, if it is immediately followed by a word or phrase set off by commas; as, The

143

engineer, who, through gross carelessness, wrecked the train, deserves the severest censure. He met with a painful accident, which, however, did not permanently injure him.

Rule 5. **An Appositive Word,** together with its adjuncts, should usually be set off by commas. Titles, when *affixed* to a noun or pronoun, should also be set off by a comma, or commas.

Gladstone, *the noted statesman*, lives in England.
Victoria, *The Queen of England*, is very wealthy.
Rev. James Russell, *D. D., LL. D.*
Harold Hunt, *Esq.*

NOTE 1. When the appositive consists of only *one* word, or only one word preceded by the article *the*, no comma is usually required; as Jesus *the Saviour* was crucified.

NOTE 2. In sentences like the following, the appositive is not set off by commas; as, Goldsmith Maid was called the queen of the turf. He was chosen king. They elected him president.

RULE 6. **The Simple Members of a Compound Sentence,** unless short and closely connected, are generally divided by commas.

EXAMPLES.

The machine is a marvel of simplicity, but its work is truly wonderful.

"Life is short and time is fleeting."—Short, no comma needed.

Be charitable, meet your obligations promptly, and you will be respected.

He speaks earnestly, and his words carry conviction with them.

NOTE. When the members have commas within themselves, a semicolon is usually placed between the members; as James, though younger, was soon noted for his fine work; but John, being lazy and indifferent, met with little success.

RULE 7. Similar Phrases forming a Series should have a comma after each phrase.

He has sailed the seas in merchantmen, government cruisers, and fleet ocean racers.

An earnest purpose, a desire to excel, and persistent application, will win success.

RULE 8. Words or Phrases in Pairs should have a comma after each pair.

Minute by minute, day by day, and week by week, the work goes on.

He has studied Latin and Greek, philosophy and chemistry, and drawing and music.

RULE 9. Similar Words in a Series should usually be separated from *each other* by commas.

Men, women, boys, and girls were there. He spoke rapidly, distinctly, and forcibly.

The sun, moon, planets, and stars are objects of earnest study.

Love, faith, hope, and charity are written on their banner.

NOTE 1. In a series of similar words no commas are required, if the connectives are all expressed. (See example 1 below.) If the connectives are *all omitted*, the words must not only be separated from each other by commas, but a comma must be placed after the last one to separate it from what follows (see example 2.)

1. Every thought and every word and every action will be brought into judgment.

2. Every thought, every word, every action, will be brought into judgment.

NOTE 2. If the terms are adjectives, no comma should be inserted between the last one and its noun, if the latter is *final* ; as, She was a kind, generous, noble woman.

RULE 10. **Independent Elements** should be set off by commas.

UNDER THE ABOVE HEAD ARE INCLUDED :

1. The nominative case independent ; as, I believe, *Mr. Secretary*, an error has been made. *James*, go at once.
2. The nominative case absolute ; as, *He being deaf*, we talked without fear of being heard.
3. Independent adverbs ; as, *Why*, how well you look.
4. Unemphatic Interjections ; as, *Oh*, how kind you are.

RULE 11. **Dependent** and **Conditional Clauses** are usually set off by commas.

EXAMPLES.

I will go early in the morning, *if I can secure a horse.*
I will not go, *unless he returns by this evening*.
Educate a man, and you increase his usefulness.

NOTE 1. In the preceding sentence the condition is implied ; the meaning being, "*If you* educate a man," etc.

NOTE 2. A clause is dependent when it requires another to complete its meaning. A dependent clause usually begins with if, unless, where, when, until, in order, etc.

NOTE 3. If the sentence is short, and the connection close, no comma should be used; as, He will come as he went. You may return when you can.

RULE 12. **Transposed Phrases** or **Clauses** placed at the beginning of a sentence, should usually be set off by a comma.

At the end of a few hours, they reached the cabin.

Hunted by every one, there seemed little chance of escape.

To tell the truth, his record was never brilliant.

To be plain, I cannot say I like it.

" *Who would be free,* themselves must strike the blow."

NOTE. In making out catalogues, and lists of names, the last name is generally written first, and a comma placed after it ; as,

> Brooks, James A.
> Luce, Messrs. E. & J.
> Hood, Dr. O. B.
> Case, Geo. M., Jr.

RULE 13. **A Short Quotation,** or a sentence resembling a quotation, should be introduced by a comma.

He said, " I will be there."

Resolved, " That we tender our thanks."

I say, " You ought not to go."

He began his speech by saying, " It is a pleasure to be with you again."

Rule 14. **The Comma should be used to prevent ambiguity,** and to make prominent emphatic or contrasted parts.

He is liberal, not lavish.   (Contrasted parts.)

The convict walked, and slept upon his bed.

> " Every lady in the land
> Has twenty nails upon each hand,
> Five and twenty upon hands and feet ;
> This is true without deceit."

" Every lady in the land
Has twenty nails ; upon each hand,
Five; and twenty upon hands and feet:
This is true without deceit. ''

———

THE SEMICOLON.

The Semicolon is used to mark the division of a sentence next longer than that indicated by the comma.

Rule 1. **Subdivided Members.** A semicolon is generally used between members that are subdivided by commas, unless the connection is very close.

EXAMPLES.

The model, though in a crude state, was exhibited a year ago ; and now, for the first time, a perfect cast has been secured.

Garfield, like Lincoln, was born of humble parents ; and, like Lincoln, was killed by an assassin's bullet while holding the highest office in the gift of the nation.

Rule 2. **Clauses and Expressions in a Series,** having a common dependence upon another clause, are separated from each other by semicolons, and from the clause upon which they depend, by a comma.

EXAMPLES.

He said, that you agreed to furnish fifty tons of coal ; that you were to deliver in five-ton lots ; and that you accepted his offer of four dollars, net.

They claim, that the instrument is superior to all others ; that it is simpler in construction ; that its action is easier and quicker ; and that its tone is fuller and richer.

NOTE. If the clause upon which the others depend, comes at the end of the sentence, it is usually separated from them by a comma, followed by a dash. Thus : " To give preference to honor above gain, when they stand in competition ;, to despise every advantage which cannot be attained without dishonest acts ; to brook no meanness; and to stoop to no dissimulations,— are the indications of a great mind.

RULE 3. **A General Term in Apposition** is usually separated from the particulars under it by a semicolon, and the particulars, from each other by commas ; as,—

He selected three books ; Pilgrim's Progress, David Copperfield, and Recreations in Astronomy.

NOTE. If the particulars contain commas within themselves, they should be separated from each other by semicolons, and from the general term by a colon ; as,—

He selected three books : Pilgrim's Progress, by Bunyan ; David Copperfield, by Dickens ; and Recreations in Astronomy, by Warren.

RULE 4. **Short Sentences,** without grammatical dependence, yet connected in meaning, are usually separated from each other by semicolons.

EXAMPLES.

The winter has gone ; the summer is here with its sunshine and flowers.

I know the morning ; I am acquainted with it and love it, fresh and sweet as it is ; a daily new creation, breaking forth and calling all that have life and breath and being to new adorations, new enjoyments, and new gratitude.—*Daniel Webster.*

NOTE. When the sentences are short, and the connection very close, a comma is generally used; as, The sun is shining, trees are budding, birds are singing ; all the earth seems glad.

149

RULE 5. **An Additional Clause.** When a clause stating a reason, explanation, or enumeration is added to a preceding sentence, it should be preceded by a semicolon, if introduced by a connecting word, but by a colon if not.

EXAMPLES.

You should gather all you can ; for it will be needed.
You should gather all you can : it will be needed.

NOTE 1. A comma is sometimes used when the sentences are very short and the connection close ; as " Be just, and fear not." " Think much, speak little."

NOTE 2. *As, namely, thus,* and *that is,* when used to connect an example with a rule, should be preceded by a semicolon, and followed by a comma; as, There are two divisions of Grammar; *namely,* Etymology and Syntax.

THE COLON.

The Colon is used to mark a division next greater than that indicated by the semicolon, and next below that of the period.

Two rules have already been given for the use of the colon, see RULE 5, also NOTE, RULE 3, under " Semicolons."

RULE 1. **Greater Divisions.** The Colon is generally used between the divisions of a sentence that are subdivided by semicolons.

EXAMPLE.

" The three great enemies to tranquility are vice, superstition and idleness : vice, which poisons and disturbs the mind with bad passions ; superstition, which fills it with imaginary terrors ; idleness, which loads it with tediousness and disgust."

RULE 2. **Direct Quotations,** if long, or formally introduced, should be preceded by a colon.

EXAMPLES.

He rose and said: "I did not come here this evening with the intention of speaking," etc.

Thomas Jefferson, in speaking of indolence, said: "Of all the cankers of human happiness, none corrodes with so silent, yet so baneful an influence as indolence.

NOTE 2. If the quotation begins a new paragraph, or if it consists of several sentences, a dash is sometimes placed after the colon.

EXAMPLE.

When the meeting was called to order, the president rose and said:—

"Gentlemen, it is with great pleasure that I introduce," etc.

RULE 3. **Yes and No.** These words should be followed by a colon when equivalent to an answer that is afterward expressed in full.

EXAMPLES.

Will he go now?　No: he cannot go now.

Are you nearly ready?　Yes, kind friend: I will soon be ready.

NOTE. In such cases as, "Yes, sir," "No, my lords," etc., the colon should come after the last word; thus, Yes, sir: I will go with you. No, my lords: I cannot agree to your proposition.

RULE 4. **The Expressions,** *as follows*, *to proceed*, *to conclude*, etc., when used to introduce an enumeration or example, or when placed at the beginning of a paragraph and referring to the whole of it, should be separated from what follows by a colon; as, To conclude: your education, in its truest, noblest sense, can never be completed.

NOTE. *Viz.* should always be preceded by a comma and followed by a colon; as, "There are three cardinal virtues, viz.: faith, hope, and charity.

RULE 5. **A Formal Salutation** in a letter; as, Dear Sir, Gentlemen, etc., should be followed by a colon, when the body of the letter begins on a line below.

EXAMPLES.

Dear Madam:
     We inclose check for balance, etc.
Gentlemen:
     Your favor is before us

NOTE. When the body of the letter follows immediately after the salutation, on the *same line*, the colon and dash are both used.

EXAMPLES.

My dear Sir:—Your favor of the, etc.
Dear Sir:—We will accept your proposition, etc.

THE PERIOD.

RULE 1. Place a period at the end of every declarative and every imperative sentence.

EXAMPLES.

James went west to Colorado.   Go at once.

RULE 2. Place a period after every abbreviation.

EXAMPLES.

M. D., for Doctor of Medicine; M. C. for member of Congress; Feb. for February; Esq. for Esquire, etc.

NOTE. When figures are used to number sections, etc., a period should be placed after the figure ; as "Three things are needed : 1. Food. 2. Clothing. 3. Medicine.

A period should also be placed after letters when used as numbers; as, Chapter XX., Verse V.

INTERROGATION POINT.

RULE 1. Place an interrogation mark after every question admitting an answer.

EXAMPLES.

When did you go ? I ask, What is to be done ?

NOTE 1. An interrogation point does not always mark the end of a sentence; as,—

The question, How shall we go ? must be decided.

NOTE 2. When several questions have a common dependence on some preceding word or clause, an interrogation point should be placed after each question ; as, When did he go ? for what purpose ? with whom ?

If, however, the word or phrase on which the series depend comes last, but one interrogation point is used, and that at the end; as, When, for what purpose, with whom did he go ?

NOTE 3. An interrogation mark is sometimes used, even though the words are not put in the form of a question ; as, You will call soon ?

THE EXCLAMATION.

The exclamation point should be used after every expression or sentence denoting *strong emotion*. What bravery ! Save me !

NOTE 1. An interjection is generally followed by an exclamation point. Unemphatic interjections either have no point after them, or else are followed by a comma. *O* seldom takes any point immediately after it.

EXAMPLES.

Alas! I am no longer rich.
Oh! it hurts.
Oh, yes: we will go.
O my country!

NOTE 2. Where the interjection forms part of the clause or expression, the exclamation point should be placed at the end of the clause or expression; as, O vain man! Oh that I could make him happy!

THE DASH.

This point is greatly misused by many, especially by young writers, and considerable care should be exercised in its use. Do not employ the dash where another point could be substituted for it without changing the meaning.

RULE 1. **Abrupt Changes** in construction or sentiment should be marked by a dash.

EXAMPLES.

Could it have been James—but no, I do not believe he would go.
He was great—in his own estimation.

RULE 2. Use the dash to denote a summing up of particulars; as, You will be supplied with paper, pens, ink, and pencil,—everything needed.
He has lost home, friends, wealth,—everything.

RULE 3. **Parenthetical Expressions,** less closely connected with the rest of the sentence than would be indicated by commas, should be inclosed in dashes; as,—

I saw—probably owing to the reflected light—the figure of a man.

" Religion—who can doubt it?—is the noblest theme for the exercise of the intellect."

RULE 4. The dash is sometimes used in the following:

1. After *as, namely, as follows,* etc., when the example, enumeration, or quotation begins a separate line. See *as,* below.

2. At the end of an extract, before the name of the author or work; as,—

The rose is finest when 'tis budding new.—*Scott.*

—

MARKS OF PARENTHESIS, ( ).

RULE 1. The curves are used to inclose words or figures inserted in a sentence by way of comment, but having little or no connection with the sentence; as,

This error (if error it were) caused the loss of twenty lives, and the destruction of much valuable property.

Please send us (if you have in stock) three dozen "Ideal" Copy Holders.

NOTE. When a point would be required between the parts of a sentence, in case no parenthesis were there, then said point should *follow the last* curve, unless there is a point *within the curves,* in which case it should *precede the first curve;* as,—

While the self-respecting man seeks the good-will of others (and there is no reason why he should not), he will not stoop to dishonorable means to obtain it.

While the self-respecting man seeks the good-will of others, (and why should he not?) he will not stoop to dishonorable means to obtain it.

QUOTATION MARKS.

RULE 1. All quoted or borrowed expressions should be enclosed in quotation marks ; as. The Bible says, "Thou shalt not steal." John said, "I will surely be there."

NOTE 1. A writer may quote words previously used by himself; as, I can only repeat what I wrote you before, "I cannot accept."

NOTE 2. Sometimes a quotation is changed somewhat; that is, the exact words are not given. In such cases the change of wording should be indicated by using only one of the quotation marks at beginning, and one at end of quotation. When the remarks of others are stated in our own language no quotation marks should be used.

NOTE 3. When a quotation is inclosed within another quotation, the inclosed one should have only single marks; as,—

I have seen it stated, "The command, 'Thou shalt not kill,' forbids many crimes besides that of murder."

When the internal quotation comes at the end, three apostrophes are used; as,—

Some one has said, " What an argument for prayer is contained in the words, 'Our Father which art in heaven!' "

Index.